Also by Robert Coover

The Origin of the Brunists

The Universal Baseball Association, J. Henry Waugh, Prop.

Pricksongs & Descants (short fictions)

A Theological Position (plays)

The Public Burning

A Political Fable

Spanking the Maid

Gerald's Party

A NIGHT AT THE MOVIES

Or, You Must Remember This

FICTIONS
BY
Robert Coover

Linden Press/Simon & Schuster
New York 1987

Copyright © 1987 by Robert Coover
All rights reserved
including the right of reproduction
in whole or in part in any form
Published by Linden Press/Simon & Schuster
A Division of Simon & Schuster, Inc.
Simon & Schuster Building
Rockefeller Center
1230 Avenue of the Americas
New York, New York 10020
LINDEN PRESS/SIMON & SCHUSTER and colophon
are trademarks of Simon & Schuster, Inc.
Designed by Carla Weise/Levavi & Levavi
Manufactured in the United States of America
1   3   5   7   9   10   8   6   4   2
Library of Congress Cataloging-in-Publication Data
Coover, Robert.
A night at the movies, or, You must remember this.

1. Moving-pictures—Fiction.   I. Title.   II. Title:
Night at the movies.   III. Title: You must remember this.
PS3553.0633N5   1987   813'.54   86-20941
ISBN: 0-671-61796-6

"After Lazarus" was originally published by Bruccoli Clark Publishers and "Charlie in the House of Rue" by Penmaen Press, both in 1980. Other fictions in the volume originally appeared in *Evergreen Review, TriQuarterly, Frank, Paris Exiles,* and *Playboy.* The author is grateful to the National Endowment for the Arts for a grant which supported the completion of this book and to Brown University for the computer services on which it was written.

Our expenses? *Rod, I think this is the middle of a beautiful friendship . . .*

PROGRAM

Ladies and Gentlemen May safely visit this Theatre as no Offensive Films are ever Shown Here

A Night at the Movies

THE PHANTOM OF THE MOVIE PALACE

"We are doomed, Professor! The planet is rushing madly toward Earth and no human power can stop it!" "Why are you telling me this?" asks the professor petulantly and sniffs his armpits. "Hmm. Excuse me, gentlemen," he adds, switching off his scientific instruments and, to their evident chagrin, turning away, "I must take my bath." But there is already an evil emperor from outer space in his bathtub. Even here then! He sits on the stool and chews his beard despondently, rubbing his fingers between his old white toes. The alien emperor, whose head looks like an overturned mop bucket, splashes water on the professor with his iron claw and emits a squeaky yet sinister cackle. "You're going to rust in there," grumbles the professor in his mounting exasperation.

The squat gangster in his derby and three-piece suit with boutonniere and pointed pocket handkerchief waddles impassively through a roomful of hard-boiled wisecracking bottle-blond floozies, dropping ashes on them from his enormous stogie and gazing from time to time at the plump bubble of fob-watch in his hand. He wears a quizzical self-absorbed expression on his face, as though to say: Ah, the miracle of it all! the mystery! the eternal illusion! And yet . . . It's understood he's a dead man, so the girls forgive him his nasty habits, blowing at their décolletages and making such vulgar remarks and noises as befit their frolicsome lot. They are less patient with the little bugger's longing for the ineffable, however, and are likely, before he's rubbed out (will he even make it across the room? no one expects this), to break into a few old party songs just to clear the air. "How about 'The Sterilized Heiress'?" someone whispers even now. "Or, 'The Angle of the Dangle!' " " 'Roll Your Buns Over!' " "Girls, girls . . . !" sighs the gangster indulgently, his stogie bobbing. " 'Blow the Candle Out!' "

The husband and wife, in response to some powerful code from the dreamtime of the race, crawl into separate beds, their only visible concession to marital passion being a tender exchange of pajamas from behind a folding screen. Beneath the snow-white sheets and chenille spreads, they stroke their strange pajamas and sing each other to sleep with songs of faith and expediency and victory in war. "My cup," the wife gasps in her chirrupy soprano as the camera closes in on her trembling lips, the luminescent gleam in her eye, "runneth over!" and her husband, eyelids fluttering as though in prayer, or perhaps the onset of sleep, replies: "Your precious voice, my love, here and yet not here, evokes for me the sweet diaphanous adjacency of presence—" (here, his voice breaks, his cheeks puff out) "—and loss!"

The handsome young priest with the boyish smile kneels against the partition and croons a song of a different sort to the nun sitting on the toilet in the next stall. A low unpleasant sound is heard; it could be anything really, even prayer. The hidden agenda here is not so much religious expression as the filmic manipulation of ingenues: the nun's only line is not one, strictly speaking, and even her faint smile seems to do her violence.

The man with the axe in his forehead steps into the flickering light. His eyes, pooled in blood, cross as though trying to see what it is that is cleaving his brain in two. His chest is pierced with a spear, his groin with a sword. He stumbles, falls into a soft plash of laughter and applause. His audience, still laughing and applauding as the light in the film flows from viewed to viewer, rises now and turns toward the exits. Which are locked. Panic ensues. Perhaps there's a fire. Up on the rippling velour, the man with the split skull is still staggering and falling, staggering and falling. *"Oh my god! Get that axe!"* someone screams, clawing at the door, and another replies: *"It's no use! It's only a rhetorical figure!" "What——?!"* This is worse than anyone thought. *"I only came for the selected short subjects!"* someone cries irrationally. They press their tear-streaked faces against the intractable doors, listening in horror to their own laughter and applause, rising now to fill the majestic old movie palace until their chests ache with it, their hands burn.

Ah, well, those were the days, the projectionist thinks, changing reels in his empty palace. The age of gold, to phrase a coin. Now the doors are always open and no one enters. His films play to a silence so profound it is not even ghostly. He still sweeps out the vast auditorium, the grand foyer and the mezzanine with their plaster statues and refreshment stands, the marble staircase, the terraced swoop of balcony, even the orchestra pit, library, rest rooms and phone booths, but all he's ever turned up is the odd candy wrapper or popcorn tub he's dropped himself. The projectionist does this intentionally, hoping one day to forget and so surprise himself with the illusion of company, but so far his memory has been discouragingly precise. All that human garbage— the chocolate mashed into the thick carpets, the kiddy-pee on the front-row seats and the gum stuck under them, sticky condoms in the balcony, the used tissues and crushed cups and toothless combs, sprung hairpins, stools clogged with sanitary napkins and water fountains with chewing gum and spittle and soggy butts— used to enrage him, but now he longs for the least sign of another's presence. Even excrement in the Bridal Fountain or black hair grease on the plush upholstery. He feels like one of those visitors to an alien planet, stumbling through endless wastelands in the vain search for life's telltale scum. A cast-out orphan in pursuit of a lost inheritance. A detective without a clue, unable even to find a crime.

Or, apropos, there's that dying hero in the old foreign legion movie (and where is that masterpiece? he should look for it, run it again some lonely night for consolation) crawling inch by inch through the infinite emptiness of the desert, turning the sand over in his fingers in the desperate hope of sifting out something—a dead weed perhaps, a mollusk shell, even a bottle cap—that might reassure him that relief, if not near at hand, at least once existed. Suddenly, off on the horizon, he sees, or seems to see, a huge luxury liner parked among the rolling dunes. He crawls aboard and finds his way to the first-class lounge, where tuxedoed gentlemen clink frosted glasses and mill about with ladies dressed in evening gowns and glittering jewels. "Water—!" he gasps hoarsely from the floor, which unexpectedly makes everyone laugh. "All right, whiskey then!" he wheezes, but the men are busy gallantly helping the ladies into lifeboats. The liner, it seems, is sinking. The men gather on the deck and sing lusty folk ballads about psychologically disturbed bandits. As the ship goes down, the foreign legionnaire, even while drowning, dies at last of thirst, a fool of sorts, a butt of his own forlorn hopes, thereby illustrating his commanding officer's earlier directive back at the post on the life of the mercenary soldier: "One must not confuse honor, gentlemen, with bloody paradox!"

The mischievous children on the screen now, utterly free of such confusions, have stolen a cooling pie, glued their teacher to her seat, burned a cat, and let an old bull loose in church. Now they are up in a barn loft, hiding from the law and plotting their next great adventure. "Why don't we set the school on fire?" suggests one of them, grinning his little freckle-faced gap-toothed grin. "Or else the truant officer?" "Or stick a hornets' nest in his helmet?" "Or in his *pants!*" They all giggle and snicker at this. "That's great! But who'll get us the hornets' nest?" They turn, smiling, toward the littlest one, squatting in the corner, smeared ear to ear with hot pie. "Kith my ath," she says around the thumb in her mouth. The gap-toothed kid claps one hand to his forehead in mock shock, rolls his eyes, and falls backwards out the loft door.

Meanwhile, or perhaps in another film, the little orphan girl, who loves them all dearly, is crawling up into the hayloft on the rickety wooden ladder. No doubt some cruel fate awaits her. This is suggested by the position of the camera, which is following close behind her, as though examining the holes in her underwear. Or perhaps those are just water spots—it's an old film. He reverses it, bringing the orphan girl's behind back down the ladder for a closer look. But it's no good. It's forever blurred, forever enigmatic. There's always this unbridgeable distance between the eye and its object. Even on the big screen.

Well, and if I *were* to bridge it, the projectionist thinks, what then? It would probably be about as definitive an experience as hugging a black hole—like all those old detective movies in which the private eye, peering ever closer, only discovers, greatly magnified, his own cankerous guilt. No, no, be happy with your foggy takes, your painted backdrops and bobbing ship models, your dying heroes spitting blood capsules, your faded ingenues in nunnery loos or up loft ladders. Or wherever she might be. In a plane crash or a chorus line or a mob at the movies, or carried off by giant apes or ants, or nuzzled by grizzlies in the white wastes of the Klondike. The miracle of artifice is miracle enough. Here she is, for example, tied to the railroad tracks, her mouth gagged, her bosom heaving as the huge engine bears down upon her. Her muffled scream blends with the train's shrieking whistle, as sound effects, lighting, motion, acting, and even set decor—the gleaming ribbons of steel rails paralleling the wet gag in her mouth, her billowing skirts echoing the distant hills—come together for a moment in one conceptual and aesthetic whole. It takes one's breath away, just as men's glimpses of the alleged divine once did, projections much less convincing than these, less inspiring of true awe and trembling.

Sometimes these flickerings on his big screen, these Purviews of Cunning Abstractions, as he likes to bill them, actually set his teeth to chattering. Maybe it's just all this lonely space with its sepulchral room presence more dreadful than mere silence, but as the footage rolls by, music swelling, guns blazing, and reels rattling, he seems to see angels up there, or something like angels, bandannas on their faces and bustles in their skirts, aglow with an eery light not of this world. Or of any other, for that matter—no, it's scarier than that. It's as though their bones (as if they had bones!) were burning from within. They seem then, no matter how randomly he's thrown the clips together, to be caught up in some terrible enchantment of continuity, as though meaning itself were pursuing them (and him! and him!), lunging and snorting at the edge of the frame, fangs bared and dripping gore.

At such times, his own projections and the monumental emptiness of the auditorium spooking him, he switches everything off, throws all the houselights on, and wanders the abandoned movie palace, investing its ornate and gilded spaces with signs of life, even if only his own. He sets the ventilators and generators humming, works the grinding lift mechanisms, opens all the fountain cocks, stirs the wisps of clouds on the dome and turns on the stars. What there are left of them. To chase the shadows, he sends the heavy ornamented curtains with their tassels and fringes and all the accompanying travelers swooping and sliding, pops on the floods and footlights, flies the screen and drops the scrim, rings the tower chimes up in the proscenium, toots the ancient ushers' bugle. There's enough power in this place to light up a small town and he uses it all, bouncing it through the palace as though blowing up a balloon. Just puzzling out the vast switchboard helps dispel those troublesome apparitions: as they fade away, his mind spreading out over the board as if being rewired—s-*pop!* flash! *whirr!*—it feels to the back of his neck like the release of an iron claw. He goes then to the mezzanine and sets the popcorn machine thupping, the cash register ringing, the ornamental fountain gurgling. He throws the big double doors open. He lets down the velvet ropes. He leans on the showtime buzzer.

There are secret rooms, too, walled off or buried under concrete during the palace's periodic transformations, and some-

times, fleeing the grander spaces, he ducks down through the
low-ceilinged maze of subterranean tunnels, snapping green and
purple sugar wafers between his teeth, the crisp translucent
wrapper crackling in his fist like the sound of fire on radio, to visit
them: old dressing rooms, kennels and stables, billiard parlors,
shower rooms, clinics, gymnasiums, hairdressing salons, garages
and practice rooms, scene shops and prop rooms, all long disused,
mirrors cracked and walls crumbling, and littered with torn post-
ers, the nibbled tatters of old theatrical costumes, mildewed
movie magazines. A ghost town within a ghost town. He raids it
for souvenirs to decorate his lonely projection booth: an
usherette's brass button, some child-star's paperdolls, old pro-
grams and ticket rolls and colored gelatin slides, gigantic letters
for the outdoor marquee. A STORY OF PASSION BLOODSHED DESIRE &
DEATH! was the last appeal he posted out there. Years ago. THE
STRANGEST LOVE A MAN HAS EVER KNOWN! DON'T GIVE AWAY THE
ENDING! The only reason he remembers is because he ran out of
D's and had to change BLOODSHED to BLOOSHED. Maybe that's why
nobody came.

He doesn't stay down here long. It's said that, beneath this
labyrinth from the remote past, there are even deeper levels,
stair-stepped linkages to all the underground burrowings of the
city, but if so, he's never found them, nor tried to. It's a kind of
Last Frontier he chooses not to explore, in spite of his compulsive
romanticism, and, sooner or later, the dark anxiety which this re-
luctance gives rise to drives him back up into the well-lit rooms
above. Red lines, painted in bygone times on the tunnel floors and
still visible, point the way back, and as he goes, nose down and
muffled in clinging shadows, he finds himself longing once more
for the homely comforts of his little projection booth. His cot and
coffeepot and the friendly pinned-up stills. His stuffed peacock
from some demolished Rivoli or Tivoli and his favorite gold ticket
chopper with the silver filigree. His bags of hard-boiled eggs and
nuts. The wonderful old slides for projecting blizzards and sand-
storms, or descending clouds for imaginary ascensions (those
were the days!), or falling roses, rising bubbles or flying fairies,

and the one that says simply (he always shouts it aloud in the echoey auditorium): "PLEASE READ THE TITLES TO YOURSELF. LOUD READING ANNOYS YOUR NEIGHBORS." Also his stacked collections of gossip columns and animation cels and Mighty Wurlitzer scores. His tattered old poster for *Hearts and Pearls: or, The Lounge-Lizard's Lost Love*, with its immemorial tag line: "The picture that could change your life!" (And it has! It has!) And all his spools and tins and bins and snippets and reels of film. Film!

Oh yes! *Adventure!* he thinks, taking the last of the stairs up to the elevator lobby two at a time and—*kfthwump!*—into the bright lights. *Comedy!* He is running through the grand foyer now, switching things off as he goes, dragging the darkness along behind him like a fluttering cape. Is everything still there? How could he have left it all behind? He clambers breathlessly up the marble staircase, his heels clocking hollowly as though chasing him, and on into the projection room tunnel, terror and excitement unfolding in his chest like a crescendo of luminous titles, rolling credits— *Romance!*

"Excuse me," the cat woman moans huskily, peering at him over her shoulder as she unzippers her skin, "while I slip into something more comfortable . . ." The superhero, his underwear bagging at the seat and knees, is just a country boy at heart, tutored to perceive all human action as good or bad, orderly or dynamic, and so doesn't know whether to shit or fly. What good is his famous X-ray vision *now?* "But—but all self-gratification only leads to tragedy!" he gasps as she presses her hot organs up against him. "Yeah? Well, hell," she whispers, blowing in his ear, "what doesn't?" Jumpin' gee-whillikers! Why does he suddenly feel like crying?

"Love!" sings the ingenue. It's her only line. She sings it again: "Love!" The film is packed edge to edge with matings or implied matings, it's hard to find her in the crowd. "Love!" There is a battle cry, a war, perhaps an invasion. Sudden explosions. Ricocheting bullets. Mob panic. "Love!" She's like a stuck record. "Love!" "*Stop!*" Bodies are tumbling off of ramparts, horses are galloping through the gates. "Love!" *"Everything's different now!"* someone screams, maybe he does. "Love!" She's incorrigible. *"Stop her, for god's sake!"* They're all shouting and shooting at *her* now with whatever they've got: arrows, cannons, death rays, blowguns, torpedoes— "Love . . . !"

The apeman, waking from a wet dream about a spider monkey and an anteater, finds himself in a strange place, protected only by a sticky breechcloth the size of a luncheon napkin, and confronted with a beautiful High Priestess, who lights up two cigarettes at once, hands him one, and murmurs: "Tell me, lard-ass, did you ever have the feeling that you wanted to go, and still have the feeling that you wanted to stay?" He is at a loss for words, having few to start with, so he steps out on the balcony to eat his cigarette. He seems to have been transported to a vast city. The little lights far below (he thinks, touching his burned tongue gingerly: Holy ancestors! The stars have fallen!) tremble as though menaced by the darkness that encases them. The High Priestess steps up behind him and runs her hand under his breechcloth. "Feeling moody, jungle boy?" World attachment, he knows, is the fruit of the tree of passion, which is the provoker of wrath as well as of desire, but he doesn't really know what to do with this knowledge, not with the exploitative hand of civilization abusing his noble innocence like this. Except maybe to yell for the elephants.

"Get away from that lever!" screams the scientist, rushing into his laboratory. But there's no one in there, he's all alone. He and all these bits and pieces of human flesh he's been stitching together over the years. There's not even a lever. That, like everything else in his mad, misguided life, is just wishful thinking. He's a complete failure and a presumptuous ass to boot. Who's he to be creating life when he can't even remember to brush his own teeth? This thing he's made is a mess. It doesn't even smell good. Probably it's all the innovations that have done him in. All these sex organs! Well, they were easier to find than brains, it's not entirely his fault, and no one can deny he did it for love. He remembers a film (or seems to: there is a montage effect) in which the

mad scientist, succeeding where he in his depressing sanity has failed, lectures his creation on the facts of life, starting with the shinbone. "The way I see it, kid, it's forget the honors, and go for the bucks." "Alas, I perceive now that the world has no meaning for those who are obliged to pass through it," replies the monster melancholically, tearing off the shinbone and crushing his creator's skull with it, "but one must act as though it might."

Perhaps it's this, he thinks, stringing up a pair of projectors at the same time, that accounts for his own stubborn romanticism—not a search for meaning, just a wistful toying with the idea of it, because: what else are you going to do with that damned bone in your hand? Sometimes, when one picture does not seem enough, he projects two, three, even several at a time, creating his own split-screen effects, montages, superimpositions. Or he uses multiple projectors to produce a flow of improbable dissolves, startling sequences of abrupt cuts and freeze frames like the stopping of a heart, disturbing juxtapositions of slow and fast speeds, fades in and out like labored breathing. Sometimes he builds thick collages of crashing vehicles or mating lovers or gun-toting soldiers, cowboys, and gangsters all banging away in unison, until the effect is like time-lapse photography of passing clouds, waves washing the shore. He'll run a hero through all the episodes of a serial at once, letting him be burned, blasted, buried, drowned, shot, run down, hung up, splashed with acid or sliced in two, all at the same time, or he'll select a favorite ingenue and assault her with a thick impasto of pirates, sailors, bandits, gypsies, mummies, Nazis, vampires, Martians, and college boys, until the terrified expressions on their respective faces pale to a kind of blurred, mystical affirmation of the universe. Which, not unexpectedly, looks a lot like stupidity. And sometimes he leaves the projector lamps off altogether, just listens in the dark to the sounds of blobs and ghouls, robots, galloping hooves and screeching tires, creaking doors, screams, gasps of pleasure and fear, hoots and snarls and blown noses, fists hitting faces and bodies pavements, arrows targets, rockets moons.

Some of these stratagems are his own inventions, others come to him through accident—a blown fuse, the keystoning rake of a tipped projector, a mislabeled film, a fly on the lens. One night he's playing with a collage of stacked-up disaster movies, for example, when the layering gets so dense the images get stuck together. When he's finally able to peel one of them loose, he finds it stripped of its cracking dam, but littered with airliner debris, molten lava, tumbling masonry, ice chunks, bowing palm trees, and a whey-faced Captain from other clips. This leads him to the idea ("What seems to be the trouble, Captain?" someone was asking, her voice hushed with dread and earnestness, as the frames slipped apart, and maybe he should have considered this question before rushing on) of sliding two or more projected images across each other like brushstrokes, painting each with the other, so to speak, such that a galloping cowboy gets in the way of some slapstick comedians and, as the films separate out, arrives at the shootout with custard on his face; or the dying heroine, emerging from montage with a circus feature, finds herself swinging by her stricken limbs from a trapeze, the arms of her weeping lover in the other frame now hugging an elephant's leg; or the young soldier, leaping bravely from his foxhole, is creamed by a college football team, while the cheerleaders, caught out in no-man's-land, get their pom-poms shot away.

He too feels suddenly like he's caught out in no-man's-land on a high trapeze with pie on his face, but he can't stop. It's too much fun. Or something like fun. He drives stampedes through upper-story hotel rooms and out the windows, moves a monster's hideous scar to a dinner plate and breaks it, beards a breast, clothes a hurricane in a tutu. He knows there's something corrupt, maybe even dangerous, about this collapsing of boundaries, but it's also liberating, augmenting his film library exponentially. And it is also necessary. The projectionist understands perfectly well that when the cocky test pilot, stunt-flying a biplane, leans out to wave to his girlfriend and discovers himself unexpectedly a mile underwater in the clutches of a giant squid, the crew from the submarine meanwhile frantically treading air a mile up the other way, the crisis they suffer—*must* suffer—is merely the elemental crisis in his own heart. It's this or nothing, guys: sink or fly!

So it is with a certain rueful yet giddy fatalism that he sweeps a cops-and-robbers film across a domestic comedy in which the goofy rattle-brained housewife is yattering away in the kitchen while serving her family breakfast. As the frames congeal, the baby gets blown right out of its highchair, the police chief, ducking a flipped pancake, gets his hand stuck in the garbage disposal, and the housewife, leaning forward to kiss her husband while telling him about her uncle's amazing cure for potato warts, drops through an open manhole. She can be heard still, carrying on her sad screwball monologue down in the city sewers somewhere, when the two films separate, the gangster, left behind in the kitchen, receiving now the husband's sleepy good-bye kiss on his way out the door to work. The hood, disgusted, whips out his gat to drill the mug (where the hell is Lefty? what happened to that goddamn bank?), but all he comes out with is a dripping egg-beater.

Lefty (if it is Lefty) is making his getaway in a hot-wired Daimler, chased through the streets of the crowded metropolis by screaming police cars, guns blazing in all directions, citizens flopping and tumbling as though the pavement were being jerked out from under them. Adjacently, cast adrift in an open boat, the glassy-eyed heroine is about to surrender her tattered virtue to the last of her fellow castaways, a bald-headed sailor with an eye-patch and a peg leg. The others watch from outside the frame, seeing what the camera sees, as the sailor leans forward to take possession of her. "Calamity is the normal circumstance of the universe," he whispers tenderly, licking the salt from her ear, as the boat bobs sensuously, "so you can't blame these poor jack-shites for having a reassuring peep at the old run-in." As her lips part in anguished submission, filling the screen, the other camera pulls back for a dramatic overview of the squealing car chase through the congested city streets: he merges the frames, sending Lefty crashing violently into the beautiful cave of her mouth, knocking out a molar and setting her gums on fire, while the sailor suddenly finds himself tonguing the side of a skyscraper, with his social finger up the city storm drains. "Shiver me timbers and strike me blind!" he cries, jerking his finger out, and the lifeboat sinks.

He recognizes in all these dislocations, of course, his lonely quest for the impossible mating, the crazy embrace of polarities, as though the distance between the terror and the comedy of the void were somehow erotic—it's a kind of pornography. No wonder the sailor asked that his eyes be plucked out! He overlays frenzy with freeze frames, the flight of rockets with the staking of the vampire's heart, Death's face with thrusting buttocks, cheesecake with chaingangs, and all just to prove to himself over and over again that nothing and everything is true. Slapstick *is* romance, heroism a dance number. Kisses kill. Back projections are the last adequate measure of freedom and great stars are clocks: no time like the presence. Nothing, like a nun with a switchblade, is happening faster and faster, and cause (that indefinable something) is a happy ending. Or maybe not.

And then . . .

THE NEXT DAY

. . . as the old titles would say, back when time wore a white hat, galloping along heroically from horizon to horizon, it happens. The realization of his worst desires. Probably he shouldn't have turned the Western on its side. A reckless practice at best, for though these creatures of the light may be free from gravity, his projectors are not: bits and pieces rattle out every time he tries it, and often as not, he ends up with a roomful of unspooled film, looping around his ears like killer ivy. But he's just begun sliding a Broadway girlie show through a barroom brawl (ah, love, he's musing, that thing of anxious fear, as the great demonic wasteland of masculine space receives the idealized thrust of feminine time), when it occurs to him in a whimsical moment to try to merge the choreography of fist and foot against face and floor by tipping the saloon scene over.

Whereupon the chorus-line ingenue, going on for the ailing star, dances out into the spotlight, all aglow with the first sweet flush of imminent stardom, only to find herself dropping goggle-eyed through a bottomless tumult of knuckles, chairs and flying bottles, sliding—*whoosh!*—down the wet bar, and disappearing feet-first through a pair of swinging doors at the bottom of the frame. Wonderful! laughs the projectionist. Worth it after all! The grizzled old prospector who's started the brawl in the first place, then passed out drunk, wakes up onstage now as the frames begin to separate in the ingenue's glossy briefs and pink ankle-strap shoes, struggling with the peculiar sensation that gravity might not know which way it wants him to fall. Thus, his knees buckle, suggesting a curtsy, even as his testicles, dangling out of the legbands of the showgirl's briefs like empty saddlebags, seem to float upward toward his ears. He opens his mouth, perhaps to sing, or else to yelp or cadge a drink, and his dentures float out like ballooned speech. "Thith ith dithgratheful!" he squawks, snatching at air as he falls in two directions at once to a standing ovation. *"Damn your eyeth!"*

Over in the saloon, meanwhile, the brawl seems to have died down. All eyes not closed by fist or drink are on the swinging doors. He rights the projector to relieve the crick in his neck from trying to watch the film sideways, noting gloomily the clunk and tinkle of tumbling parts within, wishing he might see once more that goofy bug-eyed look on the startled ingenue's face as the floor dropped out from under her. There is a brief clawed snaggle as the film rips erratically through the gate, but an expert touch of his finger on a sprocket soon restores time's main illusion. Of which there is little. The swinging doors hang motionless. Jaws gape. Eyes stare. Not much moves at all except the grinding projector reels behind him. Then slowly the camera tracks forward, the doors parting before it. The eye is met by a barren expanse of foreground mud and distant dunes, undisturbed and utterly life-less. The ingenue is gone.

He twists the knob to reverse, but something inside the machine is jammed. The image turns dark. Hastily, his hands trembling, he switches off, slaps the reels onto a spare projector, then reverses both films, sweeps them back across each other. Already changes seem to have been setting in: someone thrown out of the saloon window has been thrown back in, mouth crammed with an extra set of teeth, the stage is listing in the musical. Has he lost too much time? When the frames have separated, the old prospector has ended up back in the town saloon all right, though still in the ingenue's costume and with egg on his face, but the ingenue herself is nowhere to be seen. The ailing star, in fact, is no longer ailing, but is back in the spotlight again, belting out an old cowboy song about the saddleback image of now: *"Phantom Ri-i-i-ider!"* she bawls, switching her hips as though flicking away flies. "When stars are *bright* on a frothy *night—*"

He shuts both films down, strings up the mean gang movie with the little orphan girl in it: the water spots are there, but the loft ladder is empty! She's not in the nunnery either, the priest croons to an empty stall, as though confessing to the enthroned void— nor is she in the plummeting plane or the panicking mob or the arms, so to speak, of the blob! The train runs over a ribbon tied in a bow! The vampire sucks wind!

He turns off the projectors, listens intently. Silence, except for the faint crackle of cooling film, his heart thumping in his ears. He is afraid at first to leave his booth. What's happening out there? He heats up cold coffee on his hot plate, studies his pinned-up publicity stills. He can't find her, but maybe she was never in any of them in the first place. He's not even sure he would recognize her, a mere ingenue, if she were there—her legs maybe, but not her face. But in this cannibal picture, for example, wasn't there a girl being turned on the spit? He can't remember. And whose ripped-off heat-shield is that winged intergalactic emperor, his eyes glazed with lust and perplexity, clutching in his taloned fist? The coffee is boiling over, sizzling and popping on the burners like snapped fingers. He jerks the plug and rushes out, caroming clumsily off the doorjamb, feeling as dizzy and unhinged as that old prospector in the tights and pink pumps, not knowing which way to fall.

The cavernous auditorium, awhisper with its own echoey room presence, seems to have shrunk and expanded at the same time: the pocked dome presses down on him with its terrible finitude, even as the aisles appear to stretch away, pushing the screen toward which he stumbles further and further into the distance. "Wait!" he cries, and the stage rushes forward and slams him in the chest, knocking him back into the first row of seats. He lies there for a moment, staring up into what would be, if he could reach the switchboard, a starlit sky, recalling an old Bible epic in which the elders of a city condemned by the archangels were pleading with their unruly citizens to curb their iniquity (which looked something like a street fair with dancing girls) before it was too late. "Can't you just be friends?" they'd cried, and he wonders now: Why not? Is it possible? He's been so lonely . . .

He struggles to his feet, this archaic wish glimmering in the dark pit of his mind like a candle in an old magic lantern, and makes his way foggily up the backstage steps, doom hanging heavy over his head like the little orphan girl's water-spotted behind. He pokes around in the wings with a kind of lustful terror, hoping to find what he most fears to find. He kicks at the tassels and furbelows of the grand drapery, flounces the house curtains and travelers, examines the screen: is there a hole in it? No, it's a bit discolored here and there, threadbare in places, but much as it's always been. As are the switchboard, the banks of lights, the borders, drops, swags and tracks above. Everything seems completely normal, which the projectionist knows from his years in the trade is just about the worst situation he could be in. He tests out the house phone, pokes his nose in the empty trash barrels, braves the dusky alleyway behind the screen. And now our story takes us down this shadowed path, he murmurs to himself, feeling like a rookie cop, walking his first beat and trying to keep his chin up, danger at every strangely familiar turn, were there any in this narrow canyon. Old lines return to him like recalled catechism: She was the sort of girl who . . . Little did he know what fate . . . A few of the characters are still alive . . . He's aware of silhouettes flickering ominously just above his head—clutching hands, hatted villains, spread legs—but when he looks, they are not there. It's all in your mind, he whispers, and laughs crazily to himself. This seems to loosen him up. He relaxes. He commences to whistle a little tune.

And then he sees it. Right at nose level in the middle of his precious screen: a mad vicious scatter of little holes! His untuned whistle escapes his puckered lips like air from a punctured tire. He shrinks back. Bullet holes—?! No, not so clean as that, and the wall behind it is unmarked. It's more like someone has been standing on the other side just now, kicking at it with stiletto heels. He's almost unable to breathe. He staggers around to the front, afraid of what he'll find or see. But the stage is bare. Or maybe that *is* what he was afraid of. Uneasily, watched by all the empty seats, he approaches the holes punched out in the screen. They form crude block letters, not unlike those used on theater marquees, and what they spell out is: BEWARE THE MIDNIGHT MAN!

He gasps, and his gasp echoes whisperingly throughout the auditorium, as though the palace itself were shuddering. Its irreplaceable picture sheet is ruined. His projections will always bear this terrible signature, as though time itself were branded. He steps back, repelled—just as the huge asbestos fire curtain comes crashing down. *Wha*—?! He ducks, falls into the path of the travelers sweeping across him like silken whips. The lights are flaring and vanishing, flaring again, colors changing kaleidoscopically. He seems to see rivers ascending, clouds dropping like leaded weights. He fights his way through the swoop and swat of rippling curtains toward the switchboard, but when he arrives there's no one there. The fire curtain has been flown, the travelers are tucked decorously back in the wings like gowns in a closet. The dream cloth with its frayed metallic threads has been dropped before the screen. The house curtains are parting, the lights have dimmed. Oh no . . . !

Even as he leaps down into the auditorium and charges up the aisle, the music has begun. If it is music. It seems to be running backwards, and there are screams and honkings and wild laughter mixed in. He struggles against a rising tide of garish light, bearing down upon him from the projection booth, alive with flickering shades, beating against his body like gamma rays. "I don't need that spear, it's only a young lion!" someone rumbles through the dome, a bomb whistles, and there's a crash behind him like a huge mirror falling. "Look out! It's—*aaarrghh!*" "Sorry, ma'am!" "Great Scott, whaddaya call *that?!*" "Romance aflame through dangerous days and—" "You don't mean—?!" The uproar intensifies—*"What* awful truth?"—and his movements thicken as in a dream. He knows if he can reach the overhanging balcony lip, he can escape the projector's rake, but even as he leans against this storm of light—"I'm afraid you made one fatal mistake!" — he can feel his body, as though penetrated by an alien being from outer space, lose its will to resist. "No! No!" he cries, marveling at his own performance, and presses on through, falling momentarily blinded, into the musky shelter of the back rows.

He sprawls there in the dark, gripping a cold bolted foot, as the tempest rages on behind him, wondering: *now* what? Which calls to mind an old war film in which the two surviving crewmembers of a downed plane, finding themselves in enemy territory, disguise themselves as the front and back end of a cow to make their escape. They get caught by an enemy farmer and locked in a barn with the village bull, the old farmer muttering, "Calves or steaks! Calves or steaks!" *"Now* what?" the airman in back cries as the bull mounts them, and the one up front, sniffing the fodder, says: "Well, old buddy, I reckon that depends on whether or not you get pregnant." Such, roughly, are his own options: he can't leave, and staying may mean more than he can take. Already the thundering light is licking at his heels like an oncoming train, and he feels much like she must have felt, gagged and tied to the humming track: "Not all of us are going to come back alive, men, and before we go out there, I—" "Oh, John! Don't!" "Mad? I, who have solved the secret of life, you call me mad?" *Wheee-eeooOOOOoo-ooo!* "Please! Is *nothing* sacred?" He drags himself up the aisle, clawing desperately—"Catch me if you can, coppers!"—at the carpet, and then, driven by something like the downed airmen's craving for friendly pastures, clambers—"We

accept him, one of us, one of us . . ."—to his feet. If I can just
secure the projection booth, he thinks, lumbering forward like a
second-string heavy, maybe . . .

But he's too late. It's a disaster area. He can't even get in the
door, his way blocked by gleaming thickets of tangled film spooling out at him like some monstrous birth. He hacks his way
through to cut off the projectors, but they're not even there any
more, nothing left but the odd takeup reel, a Maltese cross or two
like dropped coins, a lens blotted with a lipsticked kiss. His
stuffed peacock, he sees through the rustling underbrush of film,
has been plucked. Gelatin slides are cooking in his coffeepot. He
stares dumbly at all this wreckage, unable to move. It's as though
his mind has got outside itself somehow, leaving his skull full of
empty room presence. Ripped-up publicity stills and organ
scores, film tins, shattered glass slides, rolls of punched tickets lie
strewn about like colossal endings. All over his pinned-up poster
for *Hearts and Pearls,* she has scribbled: FIRST THE HUNT, THEN
THE REVELS! The only publicity photo still up on the wall is the one
of the cannibals, only now someone *is* on the spit. *He* is. The spit
begins to turn. He flees, one hand clapped over his burning eyes,
the other clawing through the chattery tentacles of film that now
seem to be trying to strangle him.

He staggers into the mezzanine, stripping scraps of clinging
celluloid from his throat, his mind locked into the simplistic es-
sentials of movement and murder. He throws the light switch.
Nothing happens. The alcove lights are also dead, the newel post
lamps on the marble staircase, the chandeliers in the grand foyer.
Darkness envelops him like swirling fog, teeming with menace.
Turning to run, he slaps up against a tall column. At least, he
thinks, hanging on, it didn't fall over. The marble feels warm to
his touch and he hugs it to him as the ingenue's insane giggle rattles hollowly through the darkened palace, sweeping high over his
head like a passing wind or a plague of twittering locusts. The column seems almost to be moving, as though the whole room, like a
cyclorama, were slowly pivoting. He recalls an old movie in which
the killer finds himself trapped on a merry-go-round spinning out

of control, sparking and shrieking and hurling wooden horses into the gaping crowd like terrorists on suicide missions. The killer, too: he lets go, understanding at last as he slides helplessly across the polished terrazzo floor the eloquent implications of pratfalls. What he slams into, however, is not a gaping crowd, but the drinking fountain near the elevator lobby, its sleek ceramic skin as cold to the touch as synthetic flesh. He can hear the cavernous gurgle and splatter of water as though the fountains throughout the movie palace might be overflowing. Yes, his pants are wet and his toes feel squishy inside their shoes.

He's not far, he realizes, from the stairwell down to the rooms below, and it occurs to him, splashing over on his hands and knees (perhaps he's thinking of the bomb shelters in war movies or the motherly belly of the whale), that he might be able to hide out down there for a while. Think things out. But at the head of the stairs he feels a cold draft: he leans over and sweeps the space with his hand: The stairs are gone, he would have plummeted directly into the unchartered regions below! It's not completely dark down there, for he seems to see a dim roiling mass of ballroom dancers, drill sergeants, cartoon cats, and restless natives, like projections on smoke, vanishing even as they billow silently up toward him. Is that the ingenue among them? The one in the grass skirt, her eyes starting from their sockets? Too late. Gone, as though sucked away into the impossible chasms below.

He blinks and backs away. The room has come to a stop, a hush has descended. The water fountains are silent. The floor is dry, his pants, his shoes. Is it over? Is she gone? He finds a twist of licorice in his pocket and, without thinking, slips it between his chattering teeth. Whereupon, with a creaking noise like the opening of a closet door, a plaster statue leans out of its niche and, as he throws himself back against the wall, smashes at his feet. The licorice has disappeared. Perhaps he swallowed it whole. Perhaps it was never there. He's reminded of a film he once saw about an alien conspiracy which held its nefarious meetings in an old carnival fun house, long disused and rigged now ("now" in the film) for much nastier surprises than rolling floors and booing ghosts. The hero, trying simply to save the world, enters the fun house, only to be subjected to everything from death rays and falling masonry to iron maidens, time traps, and diabolical life-restoring machines, as though to problematize his very identity through what the chortling fun-house operators call in their otherworldly tongue "the stylistics of absence." In such a maze of probable improbability, the hero can be sure of nothing except his own inconsolable desires and his mad faith, as firm as it is burlesque, in the prevalence of secret passages. There is always, somewhere, another door. Thus, he is not surprised when, hip-deep in killer lizards and blue Mercurians, he spies dimly, far across the columned and chandeliered pit into which he's been thrown, what appears to be a rustic wooden ladder, leaning radiantly against a shadowed wall. Only the vicious gnawing at his ankles surprises him as he struggles toward it, the Mercurians' mildewed breath, the glimpse of water-spotted underwear on the ladder above him as he starts to climb. Or are those holes? He clambers upward, reaching for them, devoted as always to this passionate seizure of reality, only to have them vanish in his grasp, the ladder as well: he discovers he's about thirty feet up the grand foyer wall, holding nothing but a torn ticket stub. It's a long way back down, but he gets there right away.

He lies there on the hard terrazzo floor, crumpled up like a lounge-lizard in a gilded cage (are his legs broken? his head? *something* hurts), listening to the whisperings and twitterings high above him in the coffered ceiling, the phantasmal tinkling of the chandelier crystals, knowing that to look up there is to be lost. It's like the dockside detective put it in that misty old film about the notorious Iron Claw and the sentimental configurations of mass murder: "What's frightening is not so much being able to see only what you want to see, see, but discovering that what you think you see only because *you* want to see *it . . . sees you . . .*" As he stands there on the damp shabby waterfront in the shadow of a silent boom, watching the night fog coil in around the tugboats and barges like erotic ribbons of dream, the detective seems to see or want to see tall ghostly galleons drift in, with one-eyed pirates hanging motionless from the yardarms like pale Christmas tree decorations, and he is stabbed by a longing for danger and adventure—another door, as it were, a different dome—even as he is overswept by a paralyzing fear of the unknown. "I am menaced," he whispers, glancing up at the swaying streetlamp (but hasn't he just warned himself?), "by a darkness beyond darkness . . ." The pirates, cutlasses in hand and knives between their teeth, drop from the rigging as though to startle the indifferent barges, but even as they fall they curl into wispy shapes of dead cops and skulking pickpockets, derelicts and streetwalkers. One of them looks familiar somehow, something about the way her cigarette dances between her spectral lips like a firefly (or perhaps that *is* a firefly, the lips his perverse dream of lips) or the way her nun's habit is pasted wetly against her thighs as she fades away down a dark alley, so he follows her. She leads him, as he knew she would, into a smoky dive filled with slumming debutantes and sailors in striped shirts, where he's stopped at the door by a scarred and brooding Moroccan. "The Claw . . . ?" he murmurs gruffly into his cupped hands, lighting up. The Moroccan nods him toward the bar, a gesture not unlike that of absolution, and he drifts over, feeling a bit airy as he floats through the weary revelers, as though he might have left part of himself lying back on the docks, curled up under the swaying lamp like a piece of unspooled trailer. When he sets his revolver on the bar, he notices he can see right through it. "If it's the Claw you're after," mutters the bartender, wiping a glass nervously with a dirty rag, then falls across the bar, a knife in his back. He notices he can also see through the bartender. The barroom is empty. He's dropped his smoke somewhere. Maybe the bartender fell on it. The lights are brightening. There's a cold metallic hand in his pants. He screams. Then he realizes it's his own.

He's lying, curled up still, under the chandelier. But not in the grand foyer of his movie palace as he might have hoped. It seems to be some sort of eighteenth-century French ballroom. People in gaiters, frocks, and periwigs are dancing minuets around him, as oblivious to his presence as to the distant thup and pop of musket fire in the street. He glances up past the chandelier at the mirrored ceiling and is surprised to see, not himself, but the ingenue smiling down at him with softly parted lips, an eery light glinting magically off her snow-white teeth and glowing in the corners of her eyes like small coals, smoldering there with the fire of strange yearnings. "She is the thoroughly modern type of girl," he seems to hear someone say, "equally at home with tennis and tango, table talk and tea. Her pearly teeth, when she smiles, are marvelous. And she smiles often, for life to her seems a continuous film of enjoyment." Her smile widens even as her eyes glaze over, the glow in them burning now like twin projectors. "Wait!" he cries, but the room tips and, to the clunk and tinkle of tumbling parts, all the people in the ballroom slide out into the public square, where the Terror nets them like flopping fish.

Nor are aristocrats and mad projectionists their only catch. Other milieus slide by like dream cloths, dropping swashbucklers, cowboys, little tramps, singing families, train conductors and comedy teams, a paperboy on a bicycle, gypsies, mummies, leather-hatted pilots and wonder dogs, neglected wives, Roman soldiers in gleaming breastplates, bandits and gold diggers, and a talking jackass, all falling, together with soggy cigarette butts, publicity stills, and flattened popcorn tubs, into a soft plash of laughter and applause that he seems to have heard before. "Another fine mess!" the jackass can be heard to bray mournfully, as the mobs, jammed up behind police barricades in the dark but festive Opera House square, cry out for blood and brains. "The public is never wrong!" they scream. "Let the revels begin!"

Arc lights sweep the sky and somewhere, distantly, an ancient bugle blows, a buzzer sounds. He is pulled to his feet and prodded into line between a drunken countess and an animated pig, marching along to the thunderous piping of an unseen organ. The aisle to the guillotine, thickly carpeted, is lined with red velvet ropes and leads to a marble staircase where, on a raised platform high as a marquee, a hooded executioner awaits like a patient usher beside his gigantic ticket chopper. A voice on the public address system is recounting, above the booming organ and electrical chimes, their crimes (hauteur is mentioned, glamour, dash and daring), describing them all as "creatures of the night, a collection of the world's most astounding horrors, these abominable parvenus of iconic transactions, the shame of a nation, three centuries in the making, brought to you now in the mightiest dramatic spectacle of all the ages!" He can hear the guillotine blade rising and dropping, rising and dropping, like a link-and-claw mechanism in slow motion, the screams and cheers of the spectators cresting with each closing of the gate. "There's been some mistake!" he whimpers. If he could just reach the switchboard! Where's the EXIT sign? Isn't there always . . . ? "I don't belong here!" "Ja, zo, it iss der vages off cinema," mutters the drunken countess behind him, peeling off a garter to throw to the crowd. Spots appear on his clothing, then get left behind as he's shoved along, as though the air itself might be threadbare and discolored, and there are blinding flashes at his feet like punctures where bright light is leaking through.

"It's all in your mind," he seems to hear the usherette at the foot of the stairs whisper, as she points him up the stairs with her little flashlight, "so we're cutting it off."

"What—?!" he cries, but she is gone, a bit player to the end. The animated pig has made his stuttering farewell and the executioner is holding his head aloft like a winning lottery ticket or a bingo ball. The projectionist climbs the high marble stairs, searching for his own closing lines, but he doesn't seem to have a speaking part. "You're leaving too soon," remarks the hooded executioner without a trace of irony, as he kicks his legs out from under him. "You're going to miss the main feature." "I thought I was it," he mumbles, but the executioner, pitilessly, chooses not to hear him. He leans forward, all hopes dashed, to grip the cold bolted foot of the guillotine, and as he does so, he notices the gum stuck under it, the dropped candy wrapper, the aroma of fresh pee in plush upholstery. Company at last! he remarks wryly to himself as the blade drops, surrendering himself finally (it's a last-minute rescue of sorts) to that great stream of image-activity that characterizes the mortal condition, recalling for some reason a film he once saw (*The Revenge of Something-or-Other*, or *The Return of, The Curse of* . . .), in which—

AFTER LAZARUS

Titles and credits fade in and out against a plain white background, later understood as a bright but overcast sky. Silence at first; then, distantly, gradually augmenting, a hollow voice: *"I have risen! I have risen!"* As the cry grows louder, it repeats and echoes itself, until it folds in upon itself entirely, unfurling into a kind of hollow vibration which fades away as the last of the credits fade.

Slow even tilt down to a village on a flat plain under the overcast sky. The camera moves into the village by way of a dirt road, which gradually becomes the main street leading to the cathedral, the dominant feature of the village. The houses along the street are small, humble, huddled close together, the outer walls made of clay, some of them whitewashed. The light is penetrating but not glaring; virtually no shadows. A dark frame is painted around the doors of some houses, and there are empty flowerpots on sills or lying about. No trees, grass, flowers; no animals; everything is empty and silent. The doors are all closed, the windows shuttered. Long steady contemplative takes. The cathedral is glimpsed frequently as the camera pans slowly about, but it remains unexamined, out of focus, mere background.

Silence maintains, as the camera proceeds deeper into the village, occasionally pausing as it pans onto small streets or alleyways. These are narrower than the main street, rutted, winding. Once or twice, the camera hesitates before a side street, zooms in slightly, pauses, pulls back, pans away, continues. Finally, at one side street, no different from any of the others, it zooms in slightly, hesitates, then continues slowly to advance, leaving the main road.

Same kind of penetrating shadowless light on the side street; same silence and emptiness. The houses are, if anything, poorer and pressed even more tightly together. The camera movement, though still unhurried, is less steady as it passes over the rutted street. The camera now makes frequent turns into yet smaller side streets, each in worse condition than the last, and the camera motion becomes consequently more and more unsteady. The camera pauses briefly from time to time to focus on some small detail or other: a barred door, a shuttered window, a lone dry weed, a small fence, a rock, the texture of a clay wall.

The streets narrow, the surface worsens, and so does the jolting movement of the camera, until it is almost impossible to keep anything in focus. Stop. Inconsequential view of part of a rooftop. Brief jolting motion. Stop. Inconsequential view of the street, the corner of a house. Jolting motion. Stop. View of a house, like the others, and of the narrow space between it and the next house. In this space, between the houses, but in full light (still no shadows), a cord is strung and hanging from it is a small scrap of tattered white cloth. Pan to the house and slow zoom in: clay wall, shuttered windows, closed door. The slow zoom continues, moving in on the door and toward its handle.

Sudden brief fluttering sound, like a bat's wings, loud, breaking the silence. The camera swings back to the scrap of white cloth on the line: it droops lifelessly there as before. The camera, after hesitating, begins slowly to pan back to the door. The cloth, still in view, moves slightly (no sound): the camera pauses, pans back to the cloth, waits.

Sudden loud click, amplified alarmingly. The camera wheels sharply past the unshuttered front window to the door, still closed, zooms in on the handle, pauses. The handle does not move, but the camera, after a brief wait, begins to pan hesitatingly back toward the window, the now unshuttered window. Behind it, in the darkness, a pale gaunt face is staring out, as though in anger. Or judgment. Then the face fades back into the shadows, leaving only the darkness. The camera hesitates, then zooms very slowly in on the window.

Again the loud fluttering of cloth or wings: rapid pan to the clothesline. Focusing adjustments. The tattered piece of white cloth is motionless, but the bottom end of it is now curled back up over the cord, so that it hangs in a tattered loop.

The camera pans steadily past the shuttered window to the door, from which an old woman is now emerging. She is stooped almost double, dressed heavily in black, with thick skirts to her ankles. Her shoes, of which we see only the tips from time to time, are highly polished. A heavy black shawl, draped over her head, hides her features from view. She pulls the door to with a soft click, the same click as heard before but not so amplified, and, keeping her back to the camera, moves off down the old rutted street. The camera hesitates, then follows at a discreet distance.

The old woman hobbles along through side street after rutted side street; camera motion is erratic and the camera has some difficulty keeping her in the range of the lens. Silence, except for the sound of her feet shuffling through the dust of the street. When she turns corners, as she frequently does, the camera loses sight of her for a moment, but on making the same turn, always relocates her a few paces ahead. Almost imperceptibly, the deserted streets widen, the way improves, the motion grows more even.

Suddenly, upon turning a last corner: the cathedral steps, looming high over the camera—rapid zoom back through the open square in front of the cathedral and down the main street, until the frame encompasses the entirety of the cathedral once more. The old woman is halfway up the now-distant steps, taking each of them one by one, doubled over, holding her skirts, a slow and difficult climb. At last, she reaches the top, the cathedral doors yawn open to receive her, and she passes through them to be swallowed up by the darkness within.

Distantly, very faintly: a dull throbbing tympanic music, measured, gloomy, like the cavernous beating of a sullen but determined heart. Very slow zoom in toward the cathedral, music augmenting slightly.

Sudden close-up of the open front portals of the cathedral, a priest standing in them, the funeral music bursting in thunderingly at the same instant. The face of the priest, staring out upon the village, is that seen earlier in the window of the old woman's cottage: high-domed, pale, drawn, with thin tense lips, large eyes gazing out, perhaps in anger or judgment, or even: in terror.

To the heavy measure of the dirge, the priest, still staring straight ahead, descends the cathedral steps. The camera maintains a tight focus on the priest, but visible behind him are other people, dressed in black, moving to the same somber rhythms, carrying what is eventually seen to be a casket. Upon reaching the bottom of the steps, the priest moves across the open square and on down the main street, toward the camera.

Camera focus now moves off the priest, drifting back over his shoulder to encompass the three men, walking side by side behind him. Like the priest, they are gaunt and solemn, dressed in black robes, their faces in fact identical to that of the priest. They stare straight ahead, walking slowly to the beat of the funeral music.

Behind these three men comes the casket: huge, black, ornately carved, elegant, polished and gleaming in the pervading white light of the overcast day, held aloft on the shoulders of twelve men, six on each side. Like the priest's three assistants, they are duplicates of the priest: the same pale forehead and high cheekbones, large staring eyes, etc. They wear black suits, fresh white flowers in their lapels. They advance, under their burden, with an exaggerated rocking motion from side to side, to the cadence of the dirge. One of the pallbearers winces briefly or perhaps starts to smile and quickly suppresses it.

Behind the coffin come the mourners, all women, all stooped and covered with black shawls and thick black skirts. Dust rises and drifts about their shuffling feet, but the glitter of the toes of their hard-polished shoes is still visible through it. One of the women glances up at the camera briefly: again, the same face. There are many women following the casket, their bowed backs like a dark sea, like black sheep in a fold. One woman seems more agitated in her grief than the others, her shoulders shaking; she glances up: she is laughing, silently, or perhaps is about to sneeze. Or weep. She ducks her head again.

The camera zooms slowly back from the women and tilts up to the casket, now directly overhead, rocking back and forth. As it swings away, there is a play of lights and shadows over the detail of the carving on the side, but as it rocks back over the camera, it becomes only a massive black shape against the plain white sky.

Slow elevation of the camera until it is level with the rocking casket: it rocks away from the camera, then swings toward it. Under it, the pallbearers stare expressionlessly ahead. The coffin is lidless.

Continued elevation of the camera until it is directly over the casket, pointed down at the advancing procession. The dead man is, not surprisingly, identical to the others, though his eyes bulge a bit more starkly, seem filmed over and sightless, and his lips, dried and cracked, are pulled back over his teeth in a disconcerting death-grin. He is laid out on soft velvety cushions, dressed in formal black attire much like that of the pallbearers, a wilted white flower in his lapel. His thin white hands, the fingernails long, are crossed over his breast.

Cut to the same camera position as in the first scene after the titles, village in the middle distance, etc. The funeral procession, led by the priest and his three assistants, approaches by way of the main street out of the village. The music, having diminished abruptly at the cut, now slowly augments as the procession advances. The road is lined with mourners, all dressed in black, the women wearing black shawls, the men dressed in black suits, their heads bowed. There are hundreds of these mourners, several deep all along the road, from here near the camera all the way back to the cathedral. When any of them chances to glance up, he or she reveals a face identical to that of the priest, the pallbearers, dead man, etc. One of them seems to be biting his lip, another rolls her eyes, another's shoulders are gently shaking, etc., three or four such exceptions amid the multitudes.

The procession pulls abreast of the camera, then passes on, the music augmenting to full volume, then slowly diminishing. The camera, in the road, wheels around to follow—at extreme close range—and then pauses to allow the old women to pass by. White dust, scuffed up by their polished shoes, stirs hazily around their skirts.

As the last of the old women passes, the camera tracks along behind them, now watching from the rear as the procession with its rocking casket moves slowly toward a cluster of cypresses in the middle distance. But for these cypresses, the fields are barren. The camera follows the procession at a discreet distance, steadily at first, then slowly commencing to imitate the to-and-fro motion of the casket.

The cemetery with its cypresses is enclosed by an ancient stone wall. The procession and then the camera pass through its gate and under the lugubrious trees. The walls and cypresses seem to bend toward the center of the frame as the camera passes beneath them, then vanish in a sweep at the corners. The cemetery is littered with broken tombstones, dried wreaths, little silver frames containing photographs of the dead (again, always the same face). Weeds, flowers, grass grow wildly. The procession halts at the mouth of an open grave, freshly dug, a shovel rammed into the mounds of excavated earth, and the music, abruptly, breaks off.

Cut to a close-up of the priest's face, staring down into the open grave, the mourners filing silently into the cemetery behind him, filling it completely. There is a faint rustling sound, like that made by the wind. The camera zooms slowly back to encompass more of the cemetery: there are thousands of mourners crammed in here. They make small furtive motions with their hands at their faces, then clasp them at their breasts. The sound of the wind fades away to silence.

Now the pallbearers climb the mound of freshly dug earth with their burden, the camera tilting upwards to follow: they hover above, dark against the white sky, framed in the tops of cypress trees. A quiet unarticulated murmur begins to be heard, almost inaudible at first, then gradually augmenting. The lips of the priest and his assistants seem to be moving slightly, then they close firmly, but the murmur continues, growing louder. The priest turns his gaze upon the pallbearers and nods slightly: the murmur breaks off instantly.

Carefully, the pallbearers lower the casket, the camera tilting, following its descent. As the casket enters the open grave, the camera passes overhead and zooms in sufficiently to watch it lower, holding only the twenty-four white hands of the pallbearers in the frame with the casket. The hole itself is utterly black, seems bottomless; the shadows in and around the casket gradually deepen.

Suddenly, the hands of the corpse lift tremblingly from his chest, reach plaintively up toward the pallbearers, toward the camera. The twenty-four hands release the casket simultaneously, as if in choreographed shock, and there is a brief loud gasp, almost a cry, from the multitude of mourners. The casket drops away, disappearing instantly into the blackness, but making no sound in its fall. Before the sound of the brief gasp has faded again to silence, the camera too withdraws from its overview of the grave, assumes a position at ground level about ten feet away.

During the prolonged stillness that follows, the camera, remaining at ground level, slowly zooms in toward the lip of the grave. There is a faint scraping sound, like the sound of mice in the wall. It breaks off, begins again, breaks off, continues. Then, at last, a pale trembling hand with long fingernails emerges from the grave and clutches at the edge. A moment later, the other hand appears. It claws for a hold, discovers at last the shovel, closes around it. Scraping sound now greatly amplified. The head of the corpse appears above the grave's edge. The eyes still protrude, the lips still smile rigidly. The head pivots slowly, jerkily, like that of a wooden puppet, until it comes to stare straight at the camera. Slow withdrawing zoom. With a final effort, the corpse drags himself out of the grave, staggers to his feet, stands spare and tottering at the tip.

Suddenly, a man, a pallbearer perhaps, lunges forward, jostling the camera on the way, leaps on the corpse, and tumbles to the freshly dug earth with it. He struggles to his feet (everything momentarily is in motion), lifts the dead man above his head and hurls it, its limbs twitching violently, back into the grave. There is a deep-throated community wail, almost a scream, then silence.

Close-up of the pallbearer's face: his thin lips are pulled back from exertion, his eyes bulge slightly in excitement or horror, as he stares down into the grave. Then, slowly, he lifts his eyes and gazes about him: he is alone, the cemetery is empty.

The pallbearer stumbles to the gate of the cemetery and stares down the dusty road leading to the village. It, too, is desolate. The village lies distantly on the treeless plain, the cathedral rising above it. The pallbearer starts running down the road, limbs outflung, mouth agape, the camera following at a discreet distance. He arrives at the edge of the village, stops, peers about as though confused. The village is, as at the beginning, empty and silent under the overcast sky. He staggers toward one side street, peers down it, hurries to another. He seems to be screaming, but no sound is heard. He disappears down one of the side streets, the camera pausing to hold a view of the main street and the cathedral beyond. And now, faintly at first, but more and more clearly, the hollow voice as before, already repeating and echoing itself: *"I have risen! I have risen!"* It folds in upon itself until the words are indistinguishable, and fades away.

Cut to the tattered scrap of white cloth hanging motionless on the clothesline. Slow pan past the clay walls and shuttered windows to the door. Silence. Slow pan to the pallbearer, standing about six feet from the door, clenching and unclenching his pale fists, breathing erratically. He lunges forward, hammers on the door with his fists. This hammering is not heard, but very faintly there is the sound of a heart beating. The pallbearer rattles the shutters, bangs again on the door. He tries the handle: it opens. The sound of the heartbeat increases perceptibly. He rushes inside, the camera following.

The room is plain with white walls, a dirt floor, empty but for a chair in the middle; on the chair: a black dress and shawl. The heartbeat is now clearly audible. The pallbearer grabs up the dress, stares at it a moment, then pulls it on over his black formal suit. His movements are clumsy, overanxious, his face showing tension and fear, yet a kind of pleasure as well, and a fierce determination. Once in the dress, he throws the shawl over his head, stoops, and peers up at: the pallbearer standing before her. The pallbearer smiles faintly, nods emphatically, and runs out of the house.

In the street, the pallbearer hesitates, then bursts through the door of the next house, the camera following. Again, a plain room and clothes on a chair. And again he pulls on the dress and shawl, stoops, peers up at: the pallbearer, now grinning, almost as though in greed or lust, rubbing his thin white hands together. Heartbeat continues evenly throughout these scenes.

The pallbearer bursts into an empty room: not even a chair with clothes. But by a window, on the dirt floor, he finds a fresh white flower. Smiling faintly, he picks it up, removes the wilted flower from his own lapel, inserts the fresh one. He turns and, smiling confidently now, offers the wilted flower to: the pallbearer standing beside him.

The pallbearer pulls the shawl over his head, stoops, peers into a mirror at herself. She sees in the mirror, behind her, the pallbearer, smiling at her over her humped back.

The pallbearer sits at an empty table and fastens the fresh flower in his lapel. He turns and offers the wilted flower to the pallbearer seated beside him, who offers it to the pallbearer beside him, who in turn offers it to the pallbearer beside him. The four turn, smiling, to the pallbearer standing behind the table. He returns their smile with a slight bow, his face damp now with perspiration, and accepts the wilted flower.

A shawl. He dons it, stoops over, peers up at the pallbearer, who reaches up her skirts and pulls out another dress and shawl. He dons them, stoops beside the other old woman, peers up at the pallbearer, who reaches up her skirts and pulls out another dress and shawl. He dons them, stoops beside the other two old women, peers up at the pallbearer, who reaches up her skirts, etc. Heartbeats continue.

Cut to the street. The pallbearer is rushing feverishly in and out of houses. Occasionally, doors open behind him and old women peer out, all of them stooped and wearing black shawls.

The pallbearer arranges his tie in the mirror, turns, smiling, to accept the fresh white flower from the pallbearer, three old women looking on.

Donning a shawl, the pallbearer lifts an empty wineglass to toast the pallbearer across the table from her, also holding an empty glass. The pallbearer standing beside them pours their glasses full, bows, hurrying away, adjusting the wilted flower in his lapel.

The pallbearer, smiling wryly, hands a fresh white flower to the camera. The camera moves toward a mirror on the wall: reflected there is the pallbearer, adjusting the flower in his lapel.

The street is full of women in shawls, watching the pallbearer break into one house after another. He drops the wilted flower, races back frantically to snatch it up, tripping and tumbling over himself as he does so, then picks himself up and bursts into another house. Heartbeats augment slightly.

The pallbearer pulls on the black dress, covers his head with the shawl, peers up at the pallbearer, nods her head for him to follow. She leads him to a straw mat in one corner of the room. She settles herself upon it, glancing coquettishly up at the pallbearer, then reaches in her skirts and pulls out a clay pot full of fresh white flowers. The pallbearer, smiling, accepts a flower and crawls down over her, handing the pot of flowers up to the pallbearer, who accepts one, passes the pot on to the pallbearer, who, etc.

The room is empty. The pallbearer undoes his fly, reaches inside, pulls out a shawl and dress. Quickly, he puts them on, reaches in his skirts and pulls out a fresh white flower. Heartbeats augment.

Quick cuts of shawls, flowers, lapels, mirrors, smiles, heartbeats augmenting.

The pallbearer is dashing down side streets, running in and out of houses, filling them up. Little old women in black shawls trail behind him, dropping little patties of white flowers in their wake.

The old woman on the straw mat hands the fresh white flower to the pallbearer settling down over her, who hands his wilted one up to the pallbearer. The old woman grabs at the pants of the pallbearer with the wilted flower—laughing silently, he pulls on a black shawl, as he comes tumbling down on the old woman's face. As she falls, she tosses a fresh flower to the pallbearer coming down on them all. A motion of white flowers and faces, black clothing, heartbeats augmenting.

Cut to the street, heartbeats augmenting abruptly. The pallbearer has stopped running. He listens intently, his smile erased. The shawled women watch and listen. A vein throbs in his temple. Faintly at first, in rhythm with and then replacing the heartbeat: the funeral music again.

Startled, the pallbearer staggers back a step, then sets off running toward the sound, leaping the ruts and pits of the road, stumbling, picking himself up, lumbering on, the camera following jarringly.

The music, though still muffled, slowly augments, as the pallbearer lurches pell-mell through streets populated with his like-
nesses. When he turns corners, the camera loses him briefly,
bounces hastily ahead, picks him up again. Turning one such corner, he arrives suddenly and unexpectedly at the steps of the
cathedral. He hesitates, then bounds up the steps, taking them
two and three at a time.

Inside, the church is dark and empty. The pallbearer runs toward
the altar, the sound of hollow echoing footsteps overriding briefly
the still muted music. At the altar, he finds the rich robes of the
priest, a complication of garments. He pulls some on, removes
some, pulls on others, at last gets them in the proper order, fits
the tall miter to his head and, haughtily confronting the anxious
pallbearer, points a long white finger at the robes of one of his
assistants. The pallbearer snatches up the robes and tugs them
on, stares icily at the trembling pallbearer, ordering him to don
the next assistant's robes. He does so, points to the third assistant's robes. While the pallbearer is still struggling frantically to
pull the last robe over his head, the dirge becomes suddenly
thunderingly loud. The third assistant, now fully robed, joins
the other two behind the priest, and they begin their slow measured march out of the cathedral. The music, bouncing percus-
sively off the high walls of the empty cathedral, is echoey and
distorted.

The light of day glares through the open cathedral doors at the
far end, throwing everything this side of it into silhouette, as the
priest, the three assistants, the casket supported by two rows of
pallbearers, and the mourning old women pass slowly out and
begin their descent down the broad cathedral steps. As each figure passes through the doorway, he or she is lit up briefly before
disappearing down the steps.

Slow zoom back to the pallbearer, slumped weakly at the altar, a wilted white flower in his lapel. He watches the last of the old women vanish through the open doors. The music becomes abruptly thinner, more distant, as the last old woman leaves. The pallbearer pulls himself to his feet and staggers forward, utterly drained, his feet shuffling hollowly across the stone floor.

From the cathedral doors, the pallbearer gazes down upon the procession, proceeding slowly up the main street of the village between the files of standing mourners. As far as the camera eye can see: this double row of mourners, several persons deep on either side, their heads bowed, blurring eventually into a single line, leading toward the distant grove of cypress trees.

The pallbearer stumbles wearily down the steps and toward the procession, the camera following. The music slowly augments as he pushes past the women and up to one side of the casket. He counts the pallbearers there: six. He wades through the thick mass of trailing old women, reaches at last the other side, again counts the pallbearers: also six. He stops, frowns, staring in confusion and disbelief at the procession jostling past him. Then a light seems to dawn. He struggles forward once more and, with difficulty, clambers up on the shoulders of the nearest pallbearers: yes, the casket is empty. He glances about him, at the village, the cathedral, the old women, down at the heads of the pallbearers, over his shoulder toward the cemetery, the road lined with mourners. The casket rocks from side to side. No one seems to be noticing him. He slips over the edge and down into the casket, pokes pleasurably at the plush inner lining, runs his fingers along the ornate carvings around the sides. Timidly, he eases himself down into the cushions, folding his hands on his chest. His soft smile stretches into a wide dry-lipped grin, his eyes protrude and film over. The flower in his lapel has long since wilted. The casket, all the while, rocks from side to side below the camera's overview. The music is at full strength, resonant and clear.

Cut to the open grave at the cemetery, view from ground level over clumps of freshly spaded earth toward the gate and road, the funeral procession, led by the priest and his three assistants, approaching. The sullen hollow music, which diminished abruptly at the cut, slowly augments as the procession passes through the gates and up to the open grave. When it halts, the music ceases abruptly. A wind seems to rise, then pass away. The pallbearers with their casket proceed directly overhead, looking down on the camera. The priest glances down at the camera, then turns back to the pallbearers. A low murmuring sound has begun, augmenting rapidly. The priest nods, the pallbearers lower the casket toward the camera. Sudden blackness, the murmur ceasing abruptly. Silence. Then, in the darkness, a faint nearby scraping sound, like that of mice in a wall. Silence. Again the scraping, louder. Silence. Again the scraping, faint again. Silence.

SHOOTOUT AT GENTRY'S JUNCTION

The Mex would arrive in Gentry's Junction at 12:10. Or had arrived. Couldn't be sure. That's how it was with that damned Mex: you couldn't ever be sure. Not enough he was filthy and mean, but he was a cheating treacherous snake to boot.

Sheriff Henry Harmon grunted irritably and eased his long pointed boots to the floor. He knocked his big-bowled pipe out against one spurred heel, then fit the pipe with others in the rack on his desk. There were two empty notches and at first he couldn't remember which one the pipe belonged in, nor what had happened to the other pipe. Yeah, goddamn it, he was probably already here. It'd be just like that uncivilized varmint. The Sheriff sighed with annoyance. He stuffed a few stray papers into cubbyholes, closed the lid on his humidor, slid Belle's picture back near the pipe rack, rolled down the desktop and locked it. Damn him! He slapped his thigh with a loud angry crack. Man, he really hated that brown bastard.

He stood wearily, hitched his pants, wiped his parched mouth with the back of his broad hand. He was a big man with bullish shoulders, a tall man who stooped through doorways, peered down with severe blue eyes over lean cheekbones at the folks of Gentry's Junction. Henry Harmon. Hank. A tough honest man with clear speech and powerful hands, fast hands, fair hands and sure. There was no sun in his eyes, here in his office, but still he squinted as he stared toward the old screen door, toward Main Street of Gentry's Junction. Out there somewhere. If he was here yet. Hank knew what he had to do. A man makes his own life, okay, but once it's made, it's made.

(*The wanted unwanted Mexican he stands himself at the bar. He laughs and laughs and he drinks. He is short to the extremity, nor is he lean. Squat. Squat she is the word, and dark with brown eyes like liquid. No severe. No honest. Hee hee hee! The Mexican laughs and laughs. Honest! He carries his pants and his belt of the gun low, under his marvelous world of the bouncing belly, and when he laughs he reveals teeth of the purest gold. There is much humor and much confusion in the old saloon. The Mexican he is very adored by all the world and when he tells stories with his teeth of gold and fat lips the saloon she explodes with great laughings. More than nothing, the Mexican he tells of two things: of calentitas and putitas. Calentitas—how you say? little hot ones, no?—and putitas comprehend all the womans he knows. And the Mexican, Don Pedo the Mexican bandit, he knows very much womans. Sí, señores! He knows all the womans of the men in the saloon and many many more. The men in the saloon they are not ignorant of the knowledge of Don Pedo, yet it may be seen that they laugh in felicity with him. Perhaps it is that the men of the saloon they laugh with a bitterness that is not revealed—? Who can know? Certainly it is full of doubts, for Don Pedo is he not the very same master of revelations? One man, but, he is not laughing. He sits alone at a table and he drinks and he does not laugh in felicity when the Mexican laughs, when all they laugh. Well, it may be that the ears of this discontented man are no good. May be he is too old. The Mexican he goes to*

*behind him and plants soft brown hands on the miserable shoul-
ders. The old man does not respond, in absolute, but looks at
some distance very far. "Ah, amigo mío, that you are so sad!" exclaims Pedo the Mexican with a big fat smile. It is told by an
anonymous one present that the wife of the man she is expired in
the night. "Hey, shuddup you!" greets the Mexican. "Who you
telling? Pedo he sabe bien, no?" The laughter augments itself.
"Don Pedo always savvies!" a thin voice cries. It is Señor Gentry
the rich banquero. Señor Gentry he is white as an unplumed
chicken and with red wet eyes. All the men in the bar they assent
themselves with big laughs, for it is assumed, you know, that all
the womans die beneath the Mexican later or sooner. It is the,
how you say? the legend.)*

Hank Harmon clumped across his sheriff's office to the hat rack.
He took down his belt and holster, buckled it around his hips.
Hand moved lightly: gun was in it. He spun the silver cylinder,
peered into it. Three shells, three empties: three dead badmen.
Fit three new silver bullets in, eased the hammer into place,
slipped the gun back gently into its warm sweet-smelling hollow.
He lifted his hat off the rack and, swinging it at his side, strode
out tall and lean-legged onto the old weather-bleached wooden
porch, batting the screen door open and then closed behind him
with his hard-polished boots.

Cold blue eyes squinting against the midday sun, Hank sur-
veyed his town of Gentry's Junction. Main Street was empty.
Painted wooden buildings aglare in the sun's relentless blast, but
the windows all shut and curtained. A dry unwonted silence. Haze
of hot dust skimming off toward the shimmering horizon that en-
circled the town like the edge of a hot coin. A child's curious nose
pressed against one window across the street. Nothing else.
Empty street. Stillness. Yeah. Probably here, all right.

Where to first? Flem's general store looked empty. Door half-
closed. Damn it, Harmon liked to see activity. He liked to see men
at work, or riding sweaty into town with their pay, or lounging be-

tween chores on Flem's front porch. He liked to see women in the streets, buying things, or showing off a hat, or walking their small kids. He liked to see kids playing, getting up ballgames, chasing around with toy guns, or singing together in church. Harmon knew he was not himself a profoundly religious man, but he went to church. Things didn't seem complete unless he did. He liked that, he liked order and completeness. At church, he sang the songs and dropped coins in the plate. He knew that the profoundly religious man kept faith in the middle of things and looked out on everything else from there. There was something troublesome about that notion for Hank, something womanish and spooky. Sheriff Hank Harmon was a man, to put it plain, who had both feet on the ground.

He looked over toward Gentry's bank. Locked up. Yeah, Hank was sure now, the Mex was here. The stage was due in soon with the Judge and the Marshal. But would it make it by 12:10? Or whenever? He could only hope. Their arrival would liven the place up some. As it was now, the emptiness and the silence were oppressive. Unnatural. They were hid. The whole goddamn town. Buncha babies. Hank spat out into the dust of the street. They all knew what he had to do, but they were leaving him to do it alone. That's how it always was.

The Sheriff shrugged, clamped his big hat down over his brow. He glanced at his watch. 11:35. Any time now. Yet Hank couldn't get 12:10 out of his mind. He had put it there for some goddamn reason, and now he couldn't get it out. Well, by God, he'd meet that Mexican at 12:10 even if the sonuvabitch had been here for a hundred years. Or if he didn't come for another hundred. 12:10. Harmon made his own life. He stamped down off the porch, his spurs ringing clearly in the weighted noonday hush.

(*And where is the Mexican that infamous one? He is in the office of the Sheriff. He is crumbling cowchips into the humidor. On the desk of Sheriff Henry there is a photograph of his—cómo? sí! his calentita! the guapísima calentita of the Sheriff who names herself Belle. The Mexican with a fat stump of a pencil he traces upon the photograph his own esplendid self, Don Pedo the Mexi-can bandit, in a posture not to be misunderstood. Festive carca-jadas intrude themselves from outside the screen door where are coming together many very laughing persons of Gentry's Junc-tion. The Mexican now he empties all the cubicles and drawers of the desk into a grand mountain in the center of the office, and to this mountain he puts a match. While the papers burn them-selves, he with consummate art escribes filthy words on all the walls. He will not permit of course that the papers they burn themselves completely, oh no! He makes water on them when they are but half consumed. Hee hee hee! Now the Sheriff will al-ways ask himself what was on the other half of each fragrant piece! The little round brown Mexican bandit he is wobbling all over with delicious laughing. He makes pipi and laughs and wobbles and his golden teeth they shine gloriously in the obscure office of the Sheriff of Gentry's Junction.)*

"Awright, men, now I want you t' listen t' me!" His voice rang out clear and resonant. They stared back, blankly, irresolutely. They were scared of him, Hank knew that. He stood tall and lean as a pillar, just inside the swinging doors of the old town saloon, his wide-shouldered frame silhouetted against the glare of the out-doors. They were scared of him, but they also didn't like him. They didn't want him in here. Hank wasn't surprised, and in a way he enjoyed it. In the end, he knew he'd have to go it alone any-way. But first he had to give them their chance. They had to know afterwards where they'd failed, feel guilt for it. If they couldn't be heroes, they anyway had to learn to be men. He settled his right hand down easily on the butt of his gun. "I'm meetin' the Mex at 12:10, men. I need your help." He gazed narrow-eyed around the room at their dull flat faces. Some turned away. Or stared past him. "If we go as a group, we can take him. He'll get a trial, fair and square. Gentry's Junction will be free of him." He paused. "Otherwise, it's likely to get pretty rough. Lotta people apt to get hurt. Hurt bad."

He waited. He was aware no one would move or speak if he

didn't, and that they'd suffer until he broke it. He was aware, but he didn't care, or if he cared, it was to burn them a little with this pained silence. Hank knew for whom law and order in this town came natural. He'd start with them. One by one, all alone. In a group, they sometimes got confused about things. Like in here, for example. Others if he had to, if finally he really needed more help, he could cajole into a kind of temporary cooperation on some pretense or other. The rest, the goddamn cabbageheads of this town, had to have their arms bent. But it was easy to bend them, soft as they were, only providing the overarching structure looked solid and sure of itself. United. So that was his job now. "I'm comin' back here in fifteen minutes. I want alla you men t' be here waitin'. I want you t' have your shootin' irons strapped on and be ready t' go with me." He gazed hard at their weak faces. They looked down or away. The bartender quietly mopped the bar with a rag and avoided Hank's eyes. No one said a word. The Sheriff turned and pushed out through the old swinging doors.

(*All the world are laughing, the bar she is in a roar-up. The Mexican from behind the sad old man he is twisting on the ears of him so until they are bleeding. "Eh, amigo! Why you no laugh, eh? We all happy here! You laugh!" But still the man sits himself there, pallid and miserable, as though he no hears nothing or even feels his ears not coming away now from his head. "Pedo say: YOU LAUGH!" The soft brown fingers of the Mexican bandit they insert in the sides of the mouth of the melancholic widower. The turning-down mouth is becoming into a wide and scaring grin. All the men in the saloon they laugh with big eyes to see it. Oh! Oh! Qué susto! It is so funny! The weeping man with the prodigious grin he is a most very funny man to see! Ah . . . ! The flesh she is breaking. She is cracking down across the face from the white hair to the white throat and then away she is tearing from the skull with a peculiar very sucking sound. Only are remaining the big wet eyes in their mournful sockets. Very funny, yes, of course, but, eh . . . macabre. Yes, of truth one*

*would say, I think, macabre. The round brown Mexican he is
giggling as a young boy with the teared-away flesh bunching up
like bar rags in his fat hands. He looks at one hand and he looks
at the other hand. He laughs in himself and his grand balloon of
a belly she shakes and shakes. Ay! How comic is she the grand
balloon of a belly of the Mexican! Laughing and laughing! Hee
hee hee! Now all the persons laugh! There is a sound of little fire-
crackers and the aroma of carnivals and rodeos. Hee hee hee hee!
Who could but help not laugh with Don Pedo the Mexican, eh?
Ah, happy indeed is the life in the town saloon!*)

The big roan stood waiting in the sun. No shadows now in Gentry's Junction under the high hot sun. Sheriff Harmon unhitched
his horse and swung smoothly up into the saddle. Nearly 11:45.
Had to move. He struck sharp spurs to his big blotched chestnut
and rode at a swift easy gallop out south and west toward the
ample spread of old man Gentry, the town banker. There was no
time to lose.

Lean in the saddle rode the tall Sheriff, the hooves of his sturdy
roan popping up thick spurts of dry yellow dust. No wind to tease
the raised dust. Idly it settled. Dry. A heavy still dry day, and
Sheriff Henry Harmon was pounding through it, hoping to stir it
alive.

At Gentry's ranch, Hank pulled up, dropped quickly out of the
saddle, leaving his roan ground-reined. "He ain't here, Hank,
he's up at the saloon," said the small weary woman who stood in
the door.

"Just come from there, ma'am," said Hank coldly, and stepped
on by the woman into the house. She tried to block him, but the
Sheriff moved too fast for her. Thick carpets, best ones west of
the Alleghenies, muffled his tread, but his silver spurs rang with
alarm, sounding off the bright-polished furniture, gilt-edged mirrors, and hung portraits of the Gentry line. Hank threw open the
bedroom door, revealing the chickenhearted banker cowering
pale and damp-eyed behind it. "Awright, let's go, Gentry."

"Let the M-Mex be, Hank," he whimpered. "Don't do no g-good botherin' him—"

Harmon spat in disgust, rug or no. "I'm goin' after that Mex, Gentry. And you're goin' with me."

The banker didn't answer. Just quivered in a pale squat in that frilly bedroom there, licking his dry pinkish lips.

"Now, you listen t' me, Gentry! This town's in trouble. Real trouble. And hidin' behind women's skirts and pretendin' it ain't the case ain't gonna get us *outa* trouble!"

"I-I know, Hank, b-but—"

"Gentry, for God's sake, *stand up!*"

The banker scrambled, flushing, to his feet. Still wouldn't meet the Sheriff's eyes though. "Hank, believe me, I *do* want t' help, G-God knows—why, we worked together a l-long time now, and, but—Hank, it ain't the same, this ain't the same!" And now he *was* looking, he was looking up at Hank's cool gaze, his pink eyes were pleading— "Hank, I'm tellin' you, *it just ain't no use!*"

"Gentry, you're scared!"

"W-well, so what? So what if I am? If y-you're so all-fired fu-fulla guts, why don't you just go g-g-g-git him yourself?" The banker's eyes dropped away again, falling on an envelope stuffed full of money on the French dresser. He cast a sly quivering glance up at the Sheriff. It made Harmon sick to his stomach.

"Keep it, Gentry," he snapped. "If I have t' go after that Mex alone, goddamn it, I will. But when I'm done, there's apt t' be a few changes made in this town!" Gentry's watery eyes winced as he looked up at the Sheriff and his hand clutched at his collar as though he were cold. Harmon didn't like to make that kind of threat. Smacked of taking things into your own hands, and that wasn't the way of the law. But sometimes you had to do that. Sometimes the so-called men of this town were a bunch of stuttering goddamn crybabies. "Let's face it, Gentry, that Mex has got this town so's it's forgot what law and decency is. Everybody's layin' everybody else's women and daughters, kids and old folks is stealin' the town bare, why, it ain't safe t' cross the damned street no more. It's all fallin' apart, Gentry, and so long as I'm around here, by God, I don't mean t' let it! Am I speakin' plain enough?"

The banker nodded and dropped his eyes. He was chewing miserably on his lower lip. Pale skinny man with permanent bluish circles under his weak eyes. In crisis, as now, his nose ran and his lips pulled back, showing his incisors.

"Awright, now strop on that there gun! You be at Flem's store in fifteen minutes or you can go packin'—you and all your wife's half-breed brats!"

"Okay, Hank, okay. I-I'll be there," Gentry stammered. Bastard was nearly bawling. "D-don't rub it in. I'll be there."

Hank swung around and shoved out the door. Guys like Gentry always got him sore, broke his composure. Going out, he caught a glimpse of the missus, huddled in a corner, dressed in black, wearing a veil. What did she mean by it? Stupid woman, he couldn't stop to worry about it. Outside, the solid earth felt good beneath his stride. He mounted his roan on the run. "Come on, podnuh, we got work t' do!"

(Don Pedo the most contented Mexican he is in all the parts at once. He is burning the prairies and stealing the cattles and derailing the foolish trains. Don Pedo finds great pleasure in the life. He is never never sad. Here he is in the schoolhouse demonstrating for the little childrens the exemplary marvels of his private member. Ay, the childrens! How they all love Pedo! One whiff of the coming of the bandit and Olé! Out of their seats they leap! Out with the books! Out with do this and do that! Don Pedo! Don Pedo! More! More! The schoolteacher—or, how you say? ah, yes, the schoolmarm—the schoolmarm she participates herself too in an inprecise manner of to speak. She is gagged and bound to her desk. The Mexican he lifts the petticoats which the schoolmarm has brought in all vanity from the East, and the little childrens crowd eagerly around to discover that what she has been hiding in there. Arre! Arre! they cry out in childish excitation as the Mexican he with the grand punzón is destroying a

I-don't-know-what that the schoolmarm has been keeping in that place for years and years: POP! There she goes! Olé! The childrens roll about in imitative postures to the monumental delight of their looking elders, who press around at the doors and windows, wishing only to be possible to be childrens again. The Mexican noisily he consumes the schoolmarm's bright red apple—chomp! chomp! chomp!—to the rhythm of the conclusion of his demonstration. Or perhaps the Mexican he is rather or also in the saloon playing cards. Yes, yes, see him there! There are five aces revealing themselves on the table. Three of the aces are spades. All three of the aces of spades they lie beneath the clever fingers of the smiling gold-toothed Mexican. Señor Gentry, the rich banquero, who has lost his wife, his mother, and three of his female childrens in the disastrous wagering, he suggests with a timid smile that, ah, the Sheriff, he's been told, he has, eh, just overheard, the Sheriff is perhaps out to, p-p-pardon the expression, extuh-tuh-tuh-terminate our good friend, Señor Don Pedo, heh heh. Don Pedo the grand Mexican bandit his laughter she is exploding. Hee hee hee! Kill Pedo? Hoo haw hee! The Mexican he laughs with abundance and emits thunderously that for which he is famoso. Hooo-eee! Mercy, Don Pedo! Mercy! All the world stagger out laughing into the street fanning their noses. Or it may be that the Mexican he is in the little church to instruct the young boys how to find happiness in their choir robes of silk and elsewhere. Hee hee, así es, niños! Now, all togedder! In the loft, the plump preacher he is lamenting softly for their lost and losing souls. "Dear Father! Forgive them, for they know not how they do!" Ah, the childrens! How they all adore their Don Pedo! For Don Pedo he is indeed adorable! True, true! To the extremity!)

Sheriff Harmon reined up his sweat-streaked roan outside the small white-frame church and, swinging lightly to the ground, hitched the horse to a post. 11:50. He jogged in long lean strides up to the big double door of the church, removed his wide-brimmed hat, swept back his white hair. A red impression along his brow marked where the hat had sat. He cleared his throat and stepped brusquely on into the church. It was empty but for the preacher, the good Reverend Slough, who stood alone, seemingly waiting for him, up at the shadowy pulpit. Puffy little fellow like a feather pillow, with eyes like shotgun pellets. The Sheriff strode down the center aisle of the one-room church, down the aisle he hoped to lead Belle one day soon, and on up to the preacher.

Before Hank could get a word in, however, the preacher said: "There is great evil afoot in our community, Henry." His voice was warm and mellifluous, his dewlaps beetling out wistfully over his starchy white collar. "Gentry's Junction is in a state of sin!"

Hank nodded gravely, gazed down at his boots, back up at the preacher. "That's what I come t' talk t' you about, Rev'rend. About the community. It's forgettin' all the things that has made it great."

"Great?" The good Reverend Slough gazed down upon Sheriff Harmon from his elevated pulpit, big silvery tears welling in his tiny eyes. "It is perhaps worse than you truly know," he gasped, and then began to weep.

"I'm, uh, proud t' know I can count on you, Rev'rend," murmured Hank, somewhat taken aback by Slough's impulsive sobbing.

The wee wet eyes of the preacher peered dolefully down on the Sheriff. "Seek your salvation, Henry," he snuffled solemnly, leaning forward, "while there is still time!"

Harmon fidgeted. He didn't like the personal touch. "Well, I mean t' seek the salvation, as you put it, Rev'rend, of all of Gentry's Junction."

Reverend Slough shook his head slowly, his jowls wobbling. "Henry, my son," he said gently, and touched a handkerchief to his eyes.

"I'm goin' after the Mex in just twenty minutes. I want you there. I need you, Rev'rend."

"There is no question, Henry," sighed the preacher, straightening up and gripping the pulpit, "to which violence is the answer."

"Now wait a minute, Rev'rend. We all know what the story is

here. That Mex is the cause of this town's trouble. I mean t' get rid of the cause. It's as simple as that."

"No, the cause is here, Henry," insisted Reverend Slough, pressing a pink hand against his black-robed breast. "In each and every one of us."

"Aw, come *on* now, Rev'rend——"

"I tell you, if there be chaos and evil in this corral of sorrows, my son, it is by God's——"

"Don't call me son, Slough! Remember who you're talkin' to!"

"We are all sons of the one Father, Henry. We must live by the laws not of man but of God Almighty. Our duty is to get a rope on our wayward souls, to throw them and brand them for the Lord! We must ride herd on——"

"Cut the horseshit, Slough! I want you down at——"

"Henry Harmon! This is the camping place of the Lord! In the name of all that's holy——!"

"Shut up and listen, goddamn it!" Henry bellowed up at the preacher. "I want you in Flem's general store at twelve noon sharp—that's less than twelve minutes from now! I ain't askin' you t' wear a sidearm, so don't look so sick in the face! I just want you there as a witness. I want you t' show the riffraff of this damned town what side God's on. You hear? It's up t' us, Slough, t' hold things together!"

The Sheriff watched the words seep slowly through the damp pink flesh of the preacher's face. The beady little eyes glittered a moment, then went opaque, looked away. "You don't understand, Henry. I'm not a man of this world. But all right. All right. I'll be there."

(*Pedo: He is in the saloon? It may be. Standing toetips, eggplant of a nose pressed on the edge of the bar. Or distributing little cards at a table in that place with thick but transcendently clever brown fingers. Yes, he is very maybe in the saloon, for Don Pedo the Mexican he has an insatiable—one would say, insatiable, no?—an insatiable thirst, sí. Or it may be he is in Señor Flem's general store, perched as like a fat egg on an old barrel of crackers in there, his blade in a slab of ripe old cheese, his gold teeth glittering, for this grand Mexican bandit he has an insatiable— again the word seems possible to employ—an insatiable hunger. Or perhaps, and quite more rather, he is in the bank of Señor Gentry, standing toetips at the counter window, his gun up the nose of Señor Gentry. Señor Gentry, white as curdled milk, is most magnanimous, he is giving pronto to the happy Mexican bandit that which he the happy Mexican is requiring. And Don Pedo he requires not little for he possesses an insatiable—a fine word, insatiable!—an insatiable greed. He rolls now a hundred-dollar bill around a pouch of black powder and this he introduces indelicately into the disnuded culo of Señor Gentry, discharging the magnanimous man like a rocket into the festive streets of Gentry's Junction. Ha ha! The wit, too, she is insatiable! Or perhaps—sí, señores, now without doubts! —Don Pedo the Mexican bandit is inplanting the much-inplanted señora of Señor Gentry upon a litter of sweet green bills in that same vault of security. Ah! Ah! Adelante, hombre! That this is the most insatiable insatiable of all!)*

Once back on Main Street, Sheriff Harmon reined in his wire-tough roan and jogged along meditatively in the saddle. Five minutes yet before he'd meet the others in Flem's store. Street still as death. No sign yet of the stagecoach. He hoped they'd make it, but he knew better than to count on it. But he wasn't thinking about that. Something else had been troubling Hank for some time now. A little thing, but it ate away at him. 11:55. Five minutes. Well, damn it, it should be time enough. He jerked harshly on the reins; the roan reared. "Hah!" Hank ordered. The roan turned down a side street off the main run.

Hank swung up in front of Gentry's Junction Hotel, unmounted, hitched the horse. Inside, he walked on past the clerk with a brief nod—the Sheriff was well known in the hotel—and up the stairs. At room 1210 he hesitated, then walked on in.

Belle, that sweet taunting virgin, lay naked on her broad four-poster, scratching herself idly.

"You mighta knocked," she said dryly.

Hank flushed. "Sorry, Belle," he gulped, but he couldn't help staring at her. Man, she sure looked good. She seemed sort of pale and flushed at the same time. He remembered to push the door shut, but couldn't recollect why he had to do this other thing just now, just today. "But I—Belle, listen, I'm goin' out t' meet the Mex!"

She stared at him without emotion. That hurt him. She made no move to get up from the bed or in any other way to ease the awkwardness of the situation. "How nice," she said. "Say hello for the rest of us."

"Hey, Belle!" He took a step toward her, but, though she didn't move, he sensed a revulsion in her. Something . . . but he couldn't put his finger on it. If finger was the right word. Still her lily-white hand, that hand he'd so chastely caressed, the one meant for the golden ring he'd bought, crawled and dug there between her legs. It was a pretty thing she had there, all right, but he hadn't wanted to get introduced to it exactly like this. "Belle, dontcha see! I-I don't know if—well, if I'm comin' back. That sonuvabitch is gonna be tough. And, Belle, what I gotta know is, I mean, before I go out there, are you, has he—you know what I mean: has that goddamn Mex—?" Hank swallowed. "It's hard for me t' say it, Belle, but you know what they say about him. I gotta know." It was stupid. He wished now he hadn't come. Or at least that he hadn't asked.

"Go play cops and bandidos, Sheriff," said Belle like ice.

Hank gazed greedily on her rising and falling breasts, on her soft white belly, and the pretty wad of fur where her fingers were burrowing. Then he noticed the open window. Distantly, he heard obscene laughter. A faint odor still: the Mexican's trademark. "Belle—!" He was aghast.

"That dirty rotten Mex!" Belle sobbed suddenly and pitched over on the sheets, burying her face in the pillows, her body convulsive with weeping. The sheets where she'd been lying were one goddamn mess.

The muscles around Sheriff Harmon's mouth tightened, his eyes narrowed. He gazed one last time on Belle's bloody rear, then turned and ran out of the room, down the stairs, and on out of the Gentry's Junction Hotel.

(*Don Pedo the Mexican bandit he is famoso for many talents, but none has attracted more notices than that for which his dear mama bruja named him. No importance the occasion, the Mexican he is prepared. In that illimitable orb he maintains an infinite variety of ultimate commentaries upon any subject. Sweet or acrid, silent or with thunders, scientific or metaphysical, the Mexican touches an inner resort and the correct especies she emerges in all her ambrosian glory. His bowels intricately reply wrath with wrath, love with love, but always with a spice of obscene humor. It is never entirely satisfactory, and yet nothing is ever more satisfactory. Ay de mí! Such are our happy perplexities, no? Well, come then, Don Pedo! That we may be friends! If it must be foul, let it be sweetly foul!*)

The Sheriff pulled up at a slow bitter lope in front of Flem's general store. It was noon and the zenith sun was blistering hot. The roan dripped sweat and frothed at the mouth. Harmon swung off, tied up the animal, clumped up the steps and into the store. Flem was alone.

"Flem, I'm meetin' the Mex in ten minutes. Gentry and Slough are on the way over. District Judge and the Marshal are due in on the stagecoach." Together they could do it. Damn it, they had to! "Is it here yet?"

Flem looked up at Sheriff Harmon over a pair of rimless spectacles. He was chewing lazily on a wad of tobacco. He turned and sent a thick yellow oyster into the brass spittoon some feet away. "Nope," he drawled, "it ain't."

There was an awkward pause. Hank was troubled by Gentry's and Slough's absence. "Listen, Flem, you got some rope?"

Flem sighed, aimed another gob at the spittoon. He peered

slowly around the store. "Yep, reckon I got a piece." He sat on an old three-legged stool, poking his glasses up higher on the sloping bridge of his nose from time to time with a crooked yellow finger. "Gonna tie up the Mex, are ye?"

"That's right. *We're* gonna tie up the Mex, Flem."

"Well," drawled the old storekeeper, and turned his eye on the spittoon again. "Well."

"Now listen, Flem. You know damned well if we don't get that Mex once and for all, this town is finished. And if this town is finished, you're finished."

"Yep. Well. That's prob'ly so." Flem arched his white eyebrows, gazed wearily up at the Sheriff over his spectacles, then turned and shot some more juice spittoonward. "It ain't I don't appreciate what you're doin', Hank. The law's a good thing." He sighed, rubbed his old grizzled jaw. "Yep. It's a good thing."

Hank's fury was mounting again. But before he could come back at Flem, the door opened. Sheriff Harmon spun, the gun already in his hand. It was Slough. "I'm here, Henry. It's wrong. It's a sin against the cloth. Against the Almighty Himself. But I'm here."

Hank sighed, holstered his gun. "I'm glad you come, Rev'rend. Now all we're lackin' is Gentry and the stage." He stamped over to the door, spurs ringing, looked out. Street was empty. No, wait! There he was, creeping furtively along the edges of the buildings. That cowardly sonuvabitch. Hank turned back to the others. "Gentry's comin'." Things would work out now.

"Now listen a minnit, Hank," said the old storekeeper, shifting warily on the stool. "Ye kin have all the rope ye want. Anything else in the store ye want, too. Understand? And mebbe I'll even kinder cover you like with my old Winchester, from here inside. Mebbe, I say." He spat. "But, Sheriff, I ain't goin' out there in the street. I ain't gittin' off this stool, Hank. I'm an old man and I ain't gittin' off this stool."

Gentry had slipped quietly in through the side door. He was white as a sun-baked dog turd and all atremble. Sheriff Harmon stared as though stupefied at the three of them, at the old storekeeper, the preacher, and the doddering banker. He grunted. Maybe he ought to just get on his horse and ride out of here. If he had any place to go. He thought of Belle. "Okay," he said quietly. "Okay. We'll let easy do it. I'll meet the Mex alone and disarm him." They seemed to relax a bit at this, but no one looked at him. "You chickenshits got nothin' t' worry about. Nothin'. All I want you t' do is when I got the Mex licked, I want you t' come out together, bring some rope, and show all the other yella-bellies of this goddamn town how the cards lie. That's all. Got it?"

The three of them nodded glumly. None of them spoke. Finally, Flem said in his soft easy drawl, "I wish the stage'd come in. Bring the Judge and the Marshal. I'd feel better about it."

(Don Pedo the grand terrible Mexican he is raising up the bandanna on his fat nose, concealing his gold-tooth smile. He gives a spur to the flank of his decrepit pinto and wobbles down into the path of the speeding stagecoach. The driver, growing white, pulls hard on the reins. The dust makes clouds in the dry air, while the stagecoach with abandon she skids to a halt. Bang! Bang bang! pop the guns of the Mexican. Just for fun. Hee hee hee! The horses they rear like goats and whinny in sweaty excitation. "Ain't c-c-carryin' m-much, Don Puh-Puh-Pedo, suh!" exclaims the driver making water in his pantalones. "J-jist this!" And the stagecoach driver magnanimously (ah, this is indeed a land of magnanimity!) he extracts a box from under his seat and throws it down to Pedo. The little bandido catches the strongbox with the agility that always amazes and into one of his fat saddlebags it goes like from the arts of magic. "Eh, amigo! Who you got in dere?" he laughs, indicating a fat brown finger to the coach. "You bring Pedo calentitas fresquitas from beeg city, I think?" The driver is commencing to laugh helplessly through pressed-together teeth. "They's a—hee hee!—Judge, Pedo, and the Marshal and summa his—hoo hah! wheeze!—kin!" The Mexican he fires one shot into the air. "Hey! Allabody out! You

*wanna die like peegs! Ándale!" Two men, a woman, and a
young girl creep like mouses from the coach. The happy Mexican
he takes down his bandanna and he smiles his smile of thick lips
and gold teeth. Ay! It is ever a thing to see! One of the men he is
fat like a pear with a big black hat and curls of white hair on top
and soft lips that tremble. Without explanation he too must commence to weep and laugh through his nose at the smile of Don
Pedo the Mexican. The other man, the Marshal it must be, is tall
and erect, unmoving, with eyes of smoked glass. Eh, mierda, the
Mexican he disdains to not look at this bad milk. He observes
rather and of course the woman and the little girl. The señora of
the Marshal she is noble and grandly bosomed with long much-
speaking lashes. The child is a tender thing, and she holds to her
mama with fear and temblores. The famous belly of Don Pedo he
vibrates and bright gleams his mouth of golden teeth. There is a
sound like of tent stakes being placed and in the air a remembering of circuses. Shyly then she smiles the little one up at the
friendly Mexican. Ah! the childrens, how they all love Don—
The hand of the Marshal she flicks toward the holster. The Mexican is firing and the hand of the Marshal she is ripping away—
spluf!—at the wrist. The driver and the pear—or, one wishes to
say, the Judge—cannot it would seem stop laughing like tontos.
Perhaps it is the look on the face of the Marshal that is so comic.
It is as like he has lost something but he knows not still what.
The Mexican now provides certain instructions, and in conse-
quence, the Marshal he sits himself in blind estupor on the road
behind the coach, while the Judge ties his feet with a rope to the
behind—how you say? ax-le, no? sí—to the behind ax-le. Then
the Judge he himself attaches in the same manner, tee-hee-hee-
ing all the time like a plump imbécil bird. "Tu, la primera,"
smiles Don Pedo the adored to the timid chiquita. He displays
with a glory that cannot be denied his luminous golden teeth.
"You good one only time." Ay, Pedo! A man of genius! A man of
arts! A man of quantity and resolution! The driver and the Judge
they possess tears in their eyes from such dolorous laughter. Finally, to the deception of all the world, the Mexican he uprises*

*and draws on his pantalones, though as always he forgets them to
button. "Hey! Giddap!" he shouts, and the driver in a laughing
terror cracks the whip over the unquiet horses. The stagecoach
she is launching herself off like a lighted-up puppy into the distance, snapping the Judge and the Marshal behind like a forked
tail of the devil. The warm-blooded Mexican lover he uplifts now
with jubilation the grandly bosomed Señora the Marshal upon
his escabrous pinto, smiling with the Mexican hospitality that it
is his custom. His breath is perhaps not pure, but the blushing
lady she seems not to notice. She has twice the grandness of little
Pedo, but for that the globous bandit he smiles the more proudly.
The pinto is clopping wearily under his magnificent cargo up
into the inviting hills. The limp little girl on the road, alas, too
delicate after all, she cannot see them go.)*

The stagecoach arrived grotesquely at 12:05. Sheriff Harmon left
Slough and Gentry vomiting miserably, foolishly, at the sight and
strode in a rage toward the town saloon. He batted through the
swinging doors. Empty. He peered over the bar. No one. Not
even the goddamn bartender. He slapped the doors open again
and stepped out onto the one main street. It stretched off east and
west toward the distant horizon, a hot unbroken line. The street
was banked here by ramshackle frame buildings, mostly false
storefronts, their windows all shrouded. Seemed to be telling
Hank something. The futility of it all maybe. He sighed. He was
alone. Alone with the Mexican. But: where was the Mexican?

The Sheriff of Gentry's Junction, tall, lean, proud, his cold blue
eyes squinting into the glare of the noon sun, walked silently, utterly alone, down the dusty Main Street, the jingle of his spurs
muffled only slightly by the puffs of dust kicked up by his high
heels. Sun straight overhead. He hauled out his pocket watch.
Just a couple of minutes now to 12:10. It was on. Like it or not.
He slid the watch back into his pocket as though dropping anchor.
He felt his right hand sweat and itch.

A foul insulting odor reached his nostrils. He spun, hands at the ready. Pedo the notorious Mexican bandit sat on an old over-turned bucket about ten feet back of him in the middle of the dusty street, idly picking his teeth with a splinter of wood. He was smiling broadly around the splinter, that fat-lipped sonuvabitch, and his gold teeth gleamed blindingly in the midday sun. Hank returned icily the Mexican's hot gaze. The stinking little runt. Now that he had him here, he wasn't scared of him. With cool measured steps, aware of the multitude of hidden eyes on him, the Sheriff approached the Mexican. The Mex had something in his hands. Something that shone in the sun. Knife? Gun? A watch! The Mex was grinning and holding up a gold goddamn pocket watch! Henry recognized it. It was his own. Warily, the Sheriff accepted it. He looked: 12:09. Too soon, but to hell with it, he couldn't hold himself back. He reached down toward the Mexican to disarm him. Everything seemed wrong, but he reached down. Felt like he was reaching down into death. The goddamn Mex had let one that smelled like a tomb. Still, the bastard offered no re-sistance. Harmon drew the Mex's six-shooters out of their moldy holsters. Rusty old relics. One of them didn't even have a god-damn hammer. He pitched them away. Easy as that. He grunted. Old fraud after all. He turned to signal for Flem and the others to bring the rope. Heard a soft click. Hand flicked: *holster was empty!* Henry Harmon the Sheriff of Gentry's Junction spun and met the silver bullet from his own gun square in his handsome suntanned face.

(*Don Pedo the grand Mexican bandit away he is riding on his little pinto into the setting sun, the silver star of the Sheriff pinned on his bouncing barriga like a jewel, his saddlebags full to the top, his gold teeth capturing the last gleams of the dying red sun. Clop clop clop clop. Adiós to Gentry's Junction! Behind him, the little town he is in the most festive of roar-ups. Ay! A moment for always to remember! The storekeeper, the banker, the preacher, they swing with soft felicity from scaffolds and the whiskey he is running like blood. Flames leap into the obscuring sky and the womans scream merrily. A remarkable scene! A glorious scene! Ay de mí! How sad to depart it, eh, little pinto? But these are the things of the life, no? Pues—hee hee!—adiós! Clop clop clop clop. Red red gleams the little five-pointed star in the ultimate light of the western sun.)*

GILDA'S DREAM

It seemed to happen in a foreign country in the south somewhere. Argentina maybe: Spanish was being spoken, also German, English, Italian, French, who knows what all, so perhaps it was some other place, or no real place at all. I was in the men's washroom, doing a kind of striptease. Apparently I was very good at it. What was odd about it, though (and, by the way, about that time the war had ended, as though to make the striptease possible, or even necessary), was that I had started from the bottom up, so to speak, planning to ease myself to the top, but my face remained completely covered. Except for my eyes, which stared out and somehow, at the same time, stared back at themselves: stared, that is, at their own staring. Well, it was a washroom, there were probably mirrors. "Put the blame on dames," I proposed, arousing a general disgust. The attendant, pointing at my oddly numbered testicles (I make my own luck), called me a "peasant." Perhaps he meant well, but hadn't I just saved his life? Or somebody's anyway, it was not clear (more like shadows on the wall). Nothing was clear except for the danger I was in. I was

74

breaking into little pieces, and not all of them seemed to be my
own. "You can't rule the world, Gilda, by passing the shoe."
What? I felt haunted. Who was this man who frightened me so,
the one hiding in the stall behind the louvered door? I knew he
was watching me through the slats, because I could see myself
through his eyes. From that perspective, I was both threatening
and desirable, so I understood that the fear in the room belonged
to the room itself and not to me. Suddenly I felt free, utterly free!
I fired the washroom attendant! I shot the Germans! I tossed my
head and removed a glove, overswept by the funniest feeling—I
was back together again! But then I heard the click of the secret
weapon, and realized that my surrender to him (this had already
taken place, it was not completely decent) had disturbed the cate-
gories. I'd gambled and lost. My pride, my penis, my glove, my
enigmatic beauty, my good name, everything. There would be no
going home . . .

INSIDE THE FRAME

Dry weeds tumble across a dusty tarred street, lined by low ramshackle wooden buildings. A loosely hinged screen door bangs repetitiously; nearby a sign creaks in the wind. A thin dog passes, sniffing idly at the borders of the street. More tumbleweeds. More dull banging. Finally, a bus pulls up, its windows opaqued with dust and grease. The creaking sign is heard now but not seen. Down the street, a young woman opens a door and peers out, framed by the darkness within. There is a furtive movement on a store roof, martial music in the distance. The door of the bus opens and two men step down. After a brief discussion, one of them shoots the other. Meanwhile, a matriarchal figure waits at the gate of her house like a mediating presence, somber yet hopeful. The sound of a cash register suggests a purchase. In the distance, a riderless horse can be seen, its flanks trembling and glistening with sweat. More martial music, steadily approaching. The figure on the roof is an Indian. A tall man is holding a limp woman in his arms before a window. A couple swirl past, arms linked, singing at the tops of their voices. There is something

76

startling about this. The sky darkens as though before a storm. A richly dressed lady exits the bus, followed by her Negro servant. The Indian leaps, a knife between his teeth. Someone is crying. It is a man, seated at a dinner table with his family, seen through an open doorway. The martial music augments as a marching band comes down the street, trumpets blaring. The Negro servant lifts down several valises, trunks, and hatboxes. Watched by the gunslinger, four men stride vigorously out of one building, the door banging behind them, and enter another. Beneath the back wheel of the bus, the pinned dog lifts its head plaintively, as though searching for someone who is not present and perhaps could never be. A boy with a slingshot takes aim at an old man delivering an unheard graveside soliloquy. Before this, the distant horse was seen to neigh and shake its mane. And then the martial music abruptly ended. Now, the rich lady enters the dilapidated hotel, surrounded by attentive bellhops and followed by her Negro servant, struggling comically with the baggage. A cardplayer, angry, throws his cards in the dealer's face: trouble seems to be brewing. Somewhere a garbage lid rattles menacingly in an alleyway. All of this is surrounded by darkness. The singing couple swing past again, going the other way, dressed now in identical white tuxedos, crisply edged. Thunder and lightning. The surviving member of the marching band retrieves his battered trumpet and puts it defiantly to his crushed lips. The gunslinger turns to reboard the bus, but is held back by the grizzled old sheriff. What occurs between them is partly hidden behind six young women who, flouncing by, turn their backs in unison and flip their skirts over their heads as though to suggest in this display the terrible vulnerability of thresholds. Is there laughter in the brightly lit hotel lobby? Perhaps it's only the rain beating on tin roofs. The sheriff has shot the Indian. Or an Indian. The bus has departed and several of the doors along the street have closed. Behind one of them a tear glistens in an upturned eye. A strange-looking person walks woodenly past, crossing the rain-slicked tar, staring straight ahead, his arms held out stiffly before him. Down the street, the door opens again and a young woman peers out:

the same door as before, the same dark space within, a reassurance that is not one. Beneath the creaking sign, visible once more, a man now pulls a hat brim over his eyes and steps provisionally down off a wooden porch. There is the sound somewhere of suddenly splintering glass, a piano playing. The dog with the broken back, its search forsaken, lowers its thin head in the pounding rain. And the banging door? The banging door?

LAP DISSOLVES

She clings to the edge of the cliff, her feet kicking in the wind, the earth breaking away beneath her fingertips. There is a faint roar, as of crashing waves, far below. He struggles against his bonds, chewing at the ropes, throwing himself against the cabin door. She screams as the cliff edge crumbles, a scream swept away by the rushing wind. At last the door splinters and he smashes through, tumbling forward in his bonds, rolling and pitching toward the edge of the cliff. Her hand disappears, then reappears, snatching desperately for a fresh purchase. He staggers to his knees, his feet, plunges ahead, the ropes slipping away like a discarded newspaper as he hails the approaching bus. She lets go, takes the empty seat. Their eyes meet. "Hey, ain't I seen you somewhere before?" he says.

She smiles up at him. "Perhaps."

"I got it." He takes the cigar butt out of his mouth. "You're a hoofer over at Mike's joint."

"Hoofer?"

"Yeah—the gams was familiar, but I couldn't place the face."

She smiles again, a smile that seems to melt his knees. He grabs the leather strap overhead. "I help out over at *Father* Michael's 'joint,' as you'd say, Lefty, but—"

"Father—? *Lefty!* Wait a minute, don't tell me! You ain't that skinny little brat who useta—?" It's her stop. She rises, smiling, to leave the bus. "Hey, where ya goin'? How'm I gonna see you again?"

She pauses at the door. "I guess you'll have to catch my act at Mike's joint, Lefty." She steps down, her skirts filling with the sudden breeze of the street, and, one hand at her knees, the other holding down her fluttering wide-brimmed hat, walks quickly toward the church, glancing up at him with a mischievous smile as the bus, starting up again, overtakes and passes her. Her body seems to slide backwards, past the bus windows, slipping from frame to frame as though out of his memory—or at least out of his grasp. *"Wait!"* The driver hesitates: he jams his gat to the mug's ear—she's like his last chance (he doesn't know exactly what he means by that, but he's thinking foggily of his mother, or else of his mother in the fog), and she's gone! The feeling of inexpressible longing she has aroused gives way to something more like fear, or grief, frustration (why is it that some things in the world are so hard, while others just turn to jelly?), anger, a penetrating loathing—how could she *do* this to him? He squeezes, his eyes narrowing. Everything stops. Even, for a moment, time itself. Then, in the distance, a police whistle is heard. He takes his hands away from her throat, lets her drop, and, with a cold embittered snarl, slips away into the foggy night streets, his cape fluttering behind him with the illusory suggestion of glamour.

There is a scream, the discovery of the body, the intent expression on the detective's face as, kneeling over her, he peers out into the swirling fog: who could have done such a heinous thing? The deeper recesses of the human heart never fail to astound him. "Looks like the Strangler again, sir—a dreadful business." "Yes . . ." "Never find the bastard on a night like this, he just dissolves right into it." "We'll find him, Sergeant. And don't swear." People speak of the heart as the seat of love, but in his profession he knows better. It is a most dark and mysterious labyrinth, where cruelty, suspicion, depravity, lewdness lurk like shadowy fiends, love being merely one of their more ruthless and morbid disguises. To prowl these sewers of the heart is to crawl through hell itself. At every turning, another dismaying surprise, another ghastly atrocity. One reaches out to help and finds one's arms plunged, up to the elbows, in viscous unspeakable filth. One cries out—even a friendly "Hello!"—and is met with ghoulish laughter, the terrifying flutter of unseen wings. Yet, when all seems lost, there is always the faint glimmer of light in the distance, at first the merest pinprick, but soon a glow reflecting off the damp walls, an opening mouth, then out into sunshine and green fields, a song in his heart, indeed on his lips, and on hers, answering him across the hills, as they run toward each other, arms outspread, clothing flowing loosely in the summery breeze.

They run through fields of clover, fields of sprouting wheat, fields of waist-high grasses that brush at their bodies, through reeds, thick rushes, hanging vines. He is running through a sequoia forest, a golden desert, glittering city streets, she down mountainsides, up subway stairs, across spotlit stages and six-lane highways. Faster and faster they run, their song welling as though racing, elsewhere, toward its own destination, the backgrounds meanwhile streaking by, becoming a blur of flickering images, as if he and she in their terrible outstretched urgency were running in place, and time were blowing past them like the wind, causing her long skirts to billow, his tie to lift and flutter past his shoulder, as they stare out on the vast rolling sea from the ship's bow, arms around each other's waists, lost for a moment in their thoughts, their dreams, the prospect of a new life in the New World, or *a* new world (where exactly are they going?). "We're going home," he says, as though in reply to her unspoken (or perhaps spoken) question. "We'll never have to run again."

"It hardly seems possible," she sighs, gazing wistfully at the deepening sunset toward which they seem to be sailing.

Their reverie is rudely interrupted when pirates leap aboard, rape the woman, kill the man, and plunder and sink the ship—but not before the woman, resisting the violent advances of the peg-legged pirate captain, bites his nose off. "Whud have you dud?!" he screams, clutching the hole in his face and staggering about the sinking ship on his wooden peg. The woman, her fate sealed (already the cutlass that will decapitate her is whistling through the briny air), chews grimly, grinding the nose between her jaws like a cow chewing its cud, the sort of cow she might—in the New World and in a better, if perhaps less adventurous, life—have had, a fat old spotted cow with swollen udder and long white teats, teats to be milked much like a man is milked, though less abun-dantly. Of course, what does she know about all that, stuck out on this desolate windblown ranch (listen to it whistle, it's enough to take your head off) with her drunken old father and dimwit broth-ers, who slap her around for her milkmaid's hands, saying they'd rather fuck a knothole in an unplaned board—what's "fuck"? How will she ever know? How *can* she, cut off from all the higher things of life like finishing schools and sidewalks and floodlit movie palaces and world's fairs with sky-rides and bubble dancers and futuramas? But just wait, one day . . . ! she promises herself, tugging tearfully on the teats. She leans against Old Bossy's spot-ted flank and seems to see there before her nose a handsome young knight in shining armor, or anyway a clean suit, galloping across the shaggy prairie, dust popping at his horse's hooves, coming to swoop her up and take her away from all this, off to dazzling cities and exotic islands and gay soirees. She sees herself suddenly, as a ripple courses like music through Bossy's flank, aswirl in palatial ballrooms (the dance is in her honor!) or perhaps getting out of shining automobiles and going into restaurants with tuxedoed waiters who bend low and call her "Madame" (the milk squirting into the bucket between her legs echoes her excitement, or perhaps in some weird way *is* her excitement), or else she's at gambling tables or lawn parties, at fashion shows and horse races, or, best of all, stretched out in vast canopied beds where servants, rushing in and out, bring her all her heart's desires.

But no, no, she sees nothing at all there, all that's just wishful thinking—some things in this world are as hard and abiding as the land itself, and nothing more so than Bossy's mangy old rump, even its stink is like some foul stubborn barrier locking her forever out here on this airless prairie, a kind of thick muddy wall with rubbery teats, a putrid dike holding back the real world (of light! she thinks, of music!), a barricade of bone, a vast immovable shithouse, doorless and forlorn, an unscalable rampart humped up into the louring sky, a briary hedgerow, farting citadel, trench and fleabitten earthworks all in one, a glutinous miasma (oh! what an aching heart!), a no-man's-land, a loathsome impenetrable forest, an uncrossable torrent, a bottomless abyss, a swamp infested with the living dead, their hands clawing blindly at the hovering gloom, the air pungent with rot. He staggers through them, gasping, terrified, the quicksand sucking at his feet, toothless gums gnawing at his elbows, trying to remember how it is he ended up out here—some sort of fall, an airplane crash, an anthropological expedition gone sour, shipwreck, a wrong turn on the way to the bank? Certainly he is carrying a lot of money, a whole bucketful of it—he throws it at them and they snatch it up, stuffing it in their purulent jaws like salad, chewing raucously, the bills fluttering obscenely from their mouths and the holes in their flaking cheeks.

The money distracts them long enough for him to drag himself out of the swamp and onto higher ground, where he finds an old ramshackle clapboard house, its windows dark, door banging in the wind. He stumbles inside, slams the door shut, leans against it. He can hear them out there, scratching and belching and shedding bits and pieces of their disintegrating bodies as though appetite itself were pure abstraction, made visible in but fettered by flesh. A hand smashes through a window—he swings at it with a broom handle and it splatters apart like a clay pigeon, the wrist continuing to poke about as though in blind search of its vanished fingers. He shoves furniture up against the door and nearest windows, locates hammer and nails, rips away cupboard doors and shelves and table tops, nails them higgledy-piggledy across every opening he finds, his heart pounding. When he's done, the woman frying up pancakes and bacon at the stove says, "I *know* how you feel about traveling salesmen, dear, but wouldn't it be cheaper just to buy one of their silly little back-scratchers and forget it?" He sighs. The air seems polluted somehow, as though with artifice or laughter. Is it those people outside?

"Gee, Dad," his son pipes up, ironically admiring his handiwork, "does that mean I don't have to go to school today?"

"I'm sure you can find your usual way out of the attic window and down the drainpipe, Billy, just as though it were Saturday," replies his mother, and again there is a disturbing rattle in the air.

"Hey, come on," the father complains, "it's not funny," but he seems to be alone in this opinion. He has the terrible feeling that his marriage is collapsing, even though the bacon's as crisp as ever. Or, if not his marriage, something . . .

"Hey, Dad, that's terrific!" exclaims his daughter, coming down for breakfast. "It looks like a giant tic-tac-toe board. What's it supposed to be, some kind of tribute to hurricanes or something?"

"That's right," says the mother, "it's called 'Three Sheets to the Wind.' Now, why don't you take it down, dear, and let the dog in. She's been scratching out there for an hour."

"Wow, speaking of sheets, I had the weirdest dream last night," says the daughter, ignoring the hollow static in the air. Her father shrinks into his chair, wondering whether the problem is that no one's listening—or that everyone is. "I was in this crazy city where everything kept changing into something else all the time. A house would turn into a horse just as you walked out of it or a golf course would take off and fly or a street would become a dinner table right under your feet. You might lean against a wall and find yourself out on the edge of a cliff, or climb into a car that turned out to be the lobby of a movie theater. Some guy would walk up to you and change into a pizza or a parking meter in front of your very eyes. Billy was in it, only he was sort of like a pinball machine and to shoot a ball you had to give a jerk on his peewee."

"That's stupid! Pinball machines are *girls!*"

"Maybe that explains the bed-wetting," sighs his mother.

"You were in it, too, Mom. You were in a chorus line in a kind of scary burlesque show, in which all the dancers were collapsing into blobs and freaks. One of your breasts seemed to slip down and slide out between your legs and you kept yelling something like 'Get a bucket! Get a bucket!' Dad wasn't in the dream, at least I didn't recognize him, but somebody who was pretending to be him kept hammering on the door and saying he was 'the loving dad' and please let him in. But I knew it was just a werewolf who was trying desperately to change back into a human and couldn't. See, everything kept changing except the things that were *supposed* to change."

"Speaking of your father, where is he? Wasn't he here just a minute ago?"

"I don't know. He wasn't looking very good. Sort of vague or something."

"Oh boy! Can I have his pancakes, Mom?"

"Well, I hope he paid the mortgage this month."

"Anyway, there were these midget league baseball players who turned out to be prehistoric monsters, and all of a sudden they attacked the city, only even as they went on eating up the people, the whole thing turned into a song-and-dance act in which the leading monster did a kind of ballet with the Virgin Mary who just a minute before had been a lawn chair. The two of them got into a fight and started zapping each other with ray guns and screaming about subversion on the boundaries, but just then the ship sank and everybody fell into the sea. You could see them all floating down past these enormous buttocks that turned out to belong to a dead man in a bathtub. Don't ask me who *he* was! Well, it occurred to me suddenly that if everything else was changing I must be changing, too. I looked in a mirror and saw I could flatten my nose or pull it out to a point, push my chin up to my forehead, stretch my cheeks out like wings. Still, I felt like there was something that *wasn't* changing, I couldn't put my finger on it exactly, but it was something down inside, something I could only call *me*. In fact there *had* to be this something, I thought, or nothing else made sense. But what was it? Who was down there? I was curious, so I asked the woman I was with to tell me what she thought of when she thought of me. I told her it couldn't be anything physical, my scars or my cock or the shit-streaks in my underwear, it had to be something you couldn't touch or see. And what she said was, 'Well, I think of you as a straight shooter, Sheriff, but one who can't stop lustin' after the goddamn ineffable.' "

"She said that, hunh?"

"Yup."

"Shitfire, Sheriff, what'd you do?"

"Well, I shot her." He hacks up a gob and aims it at the spittoon. "When a woman starts askin' me to change my ways— *ptooey!*—I change women." He tosses down his drink, leans away from the bar, cocks a wary eye on the swinging doors. "But now tell me somethin', podnuh—is that just my bowels movin' or is this saloon *goin'* somewhere?!"

"I'm afraid nothing stands still for long. So, just buckle up and enjoy the ride, ma'am."

"Ma'am?!"

"Yes, we'll be there soon."

"There—?"

CHARLIE IN THE HOUSE OF RUE

: For a moment he stands there as though amazed, slap-shoes splayed, baggy trousers bunched up around his waist and tattered jacket fastidiously buttoned, there in the middle of the gleaming chandeliered hallway near the foot of a broad staircase, its polished balustrade winding above him like the frame of a formal portrait. Then he blinks, his eyelids flicking shut and open under his black derby like camera shutters. He flexes his bamboo cane, his elbows, his knees, glances around, his patch of scruffy black moustache twitching with anticipation. He bends from the waist, sniffs the large leafy plants that bank the staircase, lifts box lids, peeks behind paintings. He raps with his cane the nose of a wide-antlered deer's head mounted over a door near the stairwell, smiles toothily into the hall mirror, then tips his hat forward and dances an adroit flatfooted hopscotch on the floor, a brightly waxed checkerboard of black and white marble squares. The floor, the surfaces of the paintings, the mirrors, the polished balustrade and the crystal chandelier, all glitter with a bright source-less light. Charlie swaggers jauntily through this light, chal-

lenging a hat tree to a fight, blowing his nose on a tapestry, doff-
ing his derby to a suit of armor. He hooks his cane in his vest
pocket, offers the armor a small cigar from a box on the hall table.
No? Well. He offers himself one, accepts it, thanks the armor with
an ingratiating smile. He pats his jacket, reaches deep into his
trousers, pulls out the pockets: nothing but holes. He asks the suit
of armor for a light. No response. He leans forward, knocks on
the breastplate with his cane, jumps back in alarm, at the same
time clapping his hands on the breastplate to still the reverberations. He presses his ear to the armor, sniffs its armpits, lifts the
visor, peers in. He looks down. Up. Deeper down. He shrugs,
drops the visor: it chops off the end of his cigar. He rolls his eyes
at the truncated butt, scowls, then reopens the visor and tosses it
in, leaping back as though to escape a trap. He helps himself to a
fresh cigar, and on second thought to yet two more, one for each
ear. He is about to pocket box and all when he discovers, on the
stair landing high above him, a beautiful but strangely baleful
young woman dressed in a long white gown. Abashedly, he offers
her a cigar, while hiding the one in his hand behind his back. She
gazes past him, unseeing. He returns the box to the table, pats it,
smiles apologetically up at her, then returns the two cigars tucked
behind his ears and seemingly the one behind his back as well,
and, bowing and bobbing, tipping his derby, backs away into a
doorway and out of the hall.

He presses the door shut, wipes his brow, produces a neatly
palmed cigar, and, planting it smugly in his mouth and looking
about for a light, discovers himself in a large kitchen. There are
cupboards, sideboards, larders, pots and pans, open shelves
stacked with sparkling dishes, white teacups hanging on little
hooks. They gleam brightly in the heavy shadows that seem to
hover in the kitchen like the spectral haze of failing sight. Sau-
sages, onions, and bunches of herbs are strung from overhead
beams, and in the open hearth there is a fitfully blazing fire, over
which an iron soup kettle hangs from a pothook. Nearby: a stack
of split logs, fire tongs, a poker, a straw broom. THERE'S NO PLACE
LIKE HOME says a tiled plaque on the wall. Freshly baked custard

pies have been set out to cool on a counter, next to a set of kitchen scales and a wooden rolling pin. Charlie, counting these things as if they had fallen somehow from his raggedy pockets, is not alone in the kitchen. At a table in the middle of the room sits a large bald-headed man with thick moustaches, wide suspenders, and a bright white napkin tucked under his double chin, staring lugubriously at a steaming bowl of soup set before him. Charlie approaches the man by a circuitous little sidestep, then, still at some distance, asks simperingly for a light. The fat man does not even look up from his bowl of soup. Charlie, rocking back on the heels of his slapshoes, studies the man, the soup, the man. He tiptoes forward, sniffs the soup, wrinkles his nose. He starts to stick a finger in the soup as though to taste it, pauses, daintily removes one fingerless glove, then does poke his finger in—he jerks back in pain, pops his finger in his mouth and sucks it tearfully. A pensive look crosses his pale face. He studies his finger, sucks it again, more appreciatively. He smacks his lips, sits down beside the bald-headed man. He sprinkles a bit of salt into his palm, sniffs it, tosses it over his left shoulder, then sprinkles some into the soup. He borrows the man's spoon, slurps up a spoonful of the hot soup, adds a little more salt, tosses the salt shaker over his shoulder. He tests the soup again: still not just right. He snatches up the pepper shaker, sprinkles a bit into his palm, sniffs it—and is quickly overtaken by the urge to sneeze. He struggles against it, pressing to his upper lip his finger, then his sleeve, the pepper shaker, the spoon, the man's finger—the sneeze explodes. The soup flies up into the bald man's face. The man continues to stare sullenly at the half-empty bowl, his thick moustaches dripping now with steaming soup. Charlie, looking ill with fear, wipes the soup spoon on his tie and replaces it, slithers off his chair and backs away, tipping his hat, then turns and runs as though pursued through the nearest door.

He pulls up short. He is in a lady's boudoir. There is a profusion of mirrors and flowers and fancy clothing. A beautiful young woman, perhaps the one he has seen before out on the stair landing, is standing beside the rumpled bed, removing her negligee.

Charlie, bowing and scraping, covers his eyes with one hand and tips his hat with the other, then wheels around to exit the way he came in—but smacks up against the wall: the door is gone. He staggers back, pinching his nose as though to restore its shape, gaping in amazement at the wall. He glances surreptitiously over his shoulder: the young woman is gone. In her place, a maid in a crisp black uniform with a frilly white apron and white lace collar is bent over, making up the canopied bed. Charlie blinks, shrugs his little shrug, tips his hat debonairly to her posteriors, then, sporting his bamboo cane, struts playfully around the room. He kicks through the shoes and garters and flimsy underthings scattered over the floor, preens in the mirrors, pokes in the drawers, examines the framed photograph of a child on the dressing table, sprays the armpits of his tattered jacket with an atomizer, sprays the backside of the busy maid. She is bent over still, ignoring him, tucking in the linens. He twirls his cane and, glancing skyward, catches her hem with it and lifts her skirt. She straightens up— Charlie whips his cane away and pretends to scold it. The maid pays him no heed, bending over once more to plump up the pillows. He bobs his eyebrows roguishly and hooks the skirt again, watching it climb slowly up her glowing white thighs like a theater curtain. The lights go out. When they come on again, Charlie is standing as before, holding his cane out stiffly in front of him, the maid's skirt hanging from it like a black banner; the maid herself is now over by the dressing table, her hands crossed in front of her thighs, a big O of mock surprise on her plump lips, her soft white bloomers reflected several times over in the triptych of hinged mirrors behind. Charlie gapes at his cane and its catch, spins around to stare at the bed, the maid, the mirrors, the room. His eyes narrow. He squares his thin shoulders, hitches his baggy pants, steps forward, and the lights go out again. When they return, they find Charlie still in midstride, though with jaw gaping and eyes apop, the maid back making the bed once more, her skirt, riding up her thighs, hooked by his cane held out behind him. She is bent nearly double now and, peeking coquettishly between her knees, is twitching her behind at him. The room seems to be getting brighter and brighter. Even as he completes his stride, Charlie pivots on the planted foot and, watching the maid with wide-eyed terror as her skirt rips away, backpedals frantically out of the room.

And right on over the gleaming second-floor balustrade into the vestibule far below, snatching frantically, as his feet arc helplessly up over the railing, at anything that might save him. What he catches hold of is the end of a ribbon, tied in a bow around the waist of the pale lady on the landing—it comes unknotted like a package being opened, spooling him downward in his fall. He bounces off the mounted deer's head, jabbed in the rear by the antlers, and bellyflops onto the balustrade, sliding down it head-first, his cane stuttering along the balusters like a policeman's billy rattled on a wooden fence. There is a large porcelain vase at the bottom of the balustrade which Charlie sends flying as he plunges past, but which he somehow manages to catch, just inches from the floor, even as he falls. He clambers to his feet, sets the vase safely back on the balustrade, mops his brow, straightens his tie, leans back in exhaustion, and knocks the vase to the tiled floor, where it shatters into a thousand pieces. He gazes innocently off in the opposite direction, kicking the pieces back out of sight under the stairs, then steals a glance up at the lady. She has noticed nothing. She stares off into the distance as before, as though crushed by grief, or regret, her loosened ribbons hanging down like hopes abandoned. Charlie scratches his head, leans toward her, leans away. He waves. He blows her a kiss. He whistles through his fingers. He jumps up and down and flings his arms about. Nothing. He twirls his derby on the end of his cane, then rolls it down his arm, pops it on his head, tips it from behind. He smashes another vase. He bangs on the suit of armor. He dumps out the cigar box, puts ten cigars in his mouth at once, eats one whole. But her sad abstracted expression remains the same. He plucks a rose from a broken vase, kisses it, and tosses it up to her. It falls short, striking the balustrade below and dropping onto the deer's severed head. He snatches up another, winds up and pitches it overhand, but again it only hits the balustrade. In frustration he grabs up an armload and heaves them all at once: this time a few do reach her, but bounce off unheeded, one of them snagging in her long white skirts. He picks up one of the fallen roses and bounds up the stairs to offer it to her: he smiles, he bows, he mugs, he pleads, all to no avail. He puts the rose between his teeth, dances a wistful little arabesque around her. Unexpectedly, she reaches out dolefully and touches his face—he ducks his head shyly, steps back, and finds himself somersaulting backwards down the stairs.

At the bottom, he discovers he has swallowed the rose, thorns and all, and is no longer in the hallway. There are Oriental carpets now on the floor where he sprawls, bulky leather chairs and sofas nearby, pedestal ashtrays and classical statuary. Perhaps he has somersaulted on through another doorway. Instead of staircases, bookcases: it seems to be some kind of library. He burps, crosses his eyes, coughs up a rose petal. A chandelier with milky hemispheres like bowls of soup hangs from the molded ceiling above him, casting a shimmery glow on the rows of leather bindings, the thickly draped windows and arched doorways, the large dark paintings in their gilt frames, the blank faces of the room's multitudinous clocks. Over by the fireplace, at a two-tiered ebony trolley, stands an old man with a long white goatee, dressed in a formal black suit, pince-nez, and silk top hat, drinking alone. Charlie, plucking a thorny stem from between his teeth, considers the drinks trolley wistfully, all aglitter with its rich array of glasses and bottles. He feels the top of his head, looks around for his hat, finds he is sitting on it. He pops it out, retrieves his cane and gloves, withdraws a bent cigar from his watch-fob pocket. He tucks the cigar in his mouth and, flicking specks of dust off his shabby jacket and baggy pants, swaggers over and joins the old man at the bottles as though invited. The old man has finished his drink and is pouring himself another. Charlie simpers, dips, doffs his derby, hangs it on his cane over his shoulder, holds a glass out hopefully, but the old man, his pale face desolated by some inconsolable sorrow, ignores it. He tips back his own glass, sets it down heavily for another refill. Charlie bobs his eyebrows, purses his lips, directs the old man's attention up to the chandelier, switches glasses on him. The old man picks up the empty glass, Charlie the full one, Charlie toasts the old man, tosses down his drink. The old man studies his empty glass, sets it down, fills it up again. He glances up at Charlie over his pince-nez, and Charlie switches glasses again. He toasts the old man, flops down on the arm of the overstuffed sofa, gulps down his drink. He reshapes his bent cigar, the old man pours out another drink, Charlie switches, reaches at the same time into the old man's pocket for a box of matches. He toasts the old man, strikes a match on the seat of the old man's tuxedo trousers, tosses down his drink, lights up the cigar, drops the match into his freshly emptied glass, switches, blows a smoke ring. The old man stares dismally at the empty glass with the sodden matchstick at the bottom, as Charlie returns the matchbox to the pocket, flicking his ash in after it. The old man, sighing heavily, picks out a clean glass and fills it, Charlie making a quick exchange, loosening his tie, stretching his legs out. His big toe pokes out from a hole in the sole of his shoe: Charlie wiggles it about contentedly and, switching glasses once more, falls back into the cushions of the sofa in bleary self-satisfaction. This time, however, the old man does not stop pouring. He gazes down at Charlie through his pince-nez, his old eyes adroop with rheum and misery, and continues to empty the bottle. Charlie stumbles to his feet, grabs up another glass and holds it under the flow, drinks down the full one just in time to thrust it back under as the new glass brims over. The old man, as though transfixed, continues to pour. Charlie thrusts more glasses under the gurgling bottle, drinks off some, pours others into the old man's pockets, some into his own, empties still others over his shoulders, into the ashtrays, the fireplace, his hat, the old man's hat—but he cannot keep pace, the liquor is bubbling out of the bottle onto the trolley, the sofa, dripping down his pant legs, the old man's pant legs, puddling here and there, staining the pillows and the Oriental carpets, and all the while the old man gapes at Charlie, his frail shoulders bent, his lower lip thrust out mournfully, his eyes slowly filming over like clouded lenses. The bottle

falls from his hand. Charlie, awash inside and out, grimaces confusedly. He picks up his soggy cigar, tips his hat which is not
there. He locates it, after turning around two or three times, on
the end of his cane. He clutches at it but he cannot reach it. He
staggers about, pitching and weaving, puffing futilely on his wet
cigar, trying to reach the elusive hat on the far end of his bamboo
cane. Vases fall and smash, statues tip, their heads falling, paintings tilt. Drunkenly, Charlie grabs a bookcase for support, pulls
the whole thing down on him. He climbs out, hauling himself hand
over hand up the cane until he reaches the hat. He struggles with
the cane as though the hat were snagged by it. The old man is
standing at the trolley, emptying out another bottle. Charlie frees
the hat at last and claps it sideways onto his head. He lurches
through the room on all fours, smirking foolishly, the hat bobbing
loosely on his uncombed curls, trying to make it back to the old
man and the drinks trolley, but the floor keeps tipping him in the
other direction. Finally, it tips him backwards right out the door,
the old man in his top hat and pince-nez receding like a forlorn
leave-taker on a train platform, Charlie rising to his feet and waving his wet cigar at him in befuddled farewell.

He strikes something as he pitches backwards, his feet fly
higher than his head, his derby hovering in midair momentarily
before following its owner into what proves to be an empty bathtub. Charlie struggles boozily to right himself, slipping and sliding
in the enameled tub. He clutches a soap dish, but it breaks away.
He hauls himself up by the plug chain, grabs the edge like a man
clinging to a cliff, finally heaves himself over and onto the floor,
gasping for breath. But where is his hat? He peers tipsily into the
tub: there it is, sitting on its crown as though inviting the toss of
pennies. He shrugs, takes a grip on the edge, and dips forward
into the tub headfirst. His feet arc up, kick frantically at space, his
baggy pant legs wrinkling to his knees, exposing bare sockless
ankles. His toe waggles out the hole in the sole as though seeking
something to grab on to. At last his feet come back down, his
head up: the derby is mashed down over his nose. He staggers
about blindly, wrestling with the hat, bumps into somebody. He

apologizes, backing away, and nearly tumbles into the tub again. His hand touches something, feels its length: a toilet plunger. He holds it over his head, brings the rubber suction cup down with a blow that makes his knees buckle, lifts: it sucks the hat from his head, lifting his feet a few inches off the floor as it does so. He blinks, gazes woozily around him: the person he has bumped into, he now sees, is a burly helmeted policeman with a large handlebar moustache and a gleaming five-pointed star on his chest. The policeman is sitting on a little stool in his stocking feet, fishing with a bamboo pole in the toilet bowl. Charlie recognizes the pole: it is his own cane. He tries to take it back, but the policeman resists, puffing his cheeks out. As they struggle for possession of the cane, the line comes up out of the toilet bowl: there is a huge crab on the end of it. The crab whirls around the room on the end of the fishing line, gnashing its pincers, sweeping medicine bottles off the glass shelves, cracking the bathroom mirror, batting the dangling overhead bulb and setting it swinging, causing shadows in the room to reel and leap. Charlie and the policeman are still fighting for the cane, but they are also trying to avoid the flying crab. To no avail: with one pincer it captures the policeman's nose, with the other Charlie's. Round and round they go, frowning cross-eyed at the crab, their mouths puckered up under their moustaches, their startled faces falling in and out of the wheeling shadows. Charlie finally lets go of the cane, using both hands to pry the pincer loose from his nose. He looks for something else to attach it to, finally lifts up one of the policeman's stockinged feet and clamps the pincer to the big toe. The policeman hops about now on one foot, helplessly hooked by the other to his nose, surrendering the cane so as to hold his foot up and save his nose from being torn away. Charlie twirls the cane victoriously, brushes himself off and straightens his hat and tie, primps drunkenly in the broken mirror, struggling to find himself in the multiple images and whirling shadows. As, burping, he turns to leave, he spies the toilet plunger. He picks it up and with a tender inebriated smile shows it to the hapless policeman. Perhaps the policeman hopes for a rescue. He seems to nod, his foot bobbing

with his head. Charlie lifts the policeman's helmet off, raps him on
the head with the plunger handle, sets the helmet back in place
but over the policeman's eyes. He stamps on the hopping foot and
tickles the other, then lifts the policeman's flopping coattails and
whops the plunger onto his backside, where it sticks fast, wagging
about like a stiff wooden tail, signaling Charlie, smugly chewing
on his wet cigar, toward his exit.

In the next room, the kitchen, as it happens, he weaves over to
the fireplace, where the soup kettle is still on the boil, and, bending primly from the waist, pokes his face into the fire to light his
cigar. When he pulls back, his face is smudged and his moustache
and eyebrows are smoking, but the cigar remains unlit. He scowls
muzzily at the soggy butt, wrings it out, shrugs, mashes it out on
the nearest clean white surface to hand—which turns out to be
the bald pate of the fat man at the kitchen table: he slumps there
as before, staring darkly at his bowl of soup, seemingly seething
with fury, the wet cigar smeared like a tatty toupee across his
barren dome. Charlie twitches in several directions at once, as
though trying to run but not knowing which way to go. In despera-
tion, he snatches up the straw broom and sweeps the cigar off the
man's head. It falls in the soup. Charlie stares in horror at the
thick lump of mangled cigar floating in the man's soup. He hurls
the broom over his left shoulder into the dish cupboards, grabs up
the soup bowl, lurches drunkenly to the fireplace, throws the con-
tents into the fire, ladles out another bowlful from the kettle,
pouring hot soup down his pant leg in haste, hops back anxiously
on one foot, trips and falls, spilling the soup, scrambles to his feet
and rushes back to the kettle, refills the bowl, returns cautiously,
bowl shaking in his hands, spills it in the fat man's lap, dashes
back to the kettle, beginning to delight now in all this to-ing and
fro-ing, returns to spill soup all over the table, hippety-hops back
giddily for another bowlful, hardly pausing at the kettle, dances to
the table and pours the soup on the man's head. He whips the
napkin out from under the man's chin and towels the dripping
pate, blowing on it and polishing it with his sleeve, then returns
for more soup and, with a graceful flourish, the napkin folded

crisply over his arm, plants the steaming bowl in front of the man, pirouettes with outflung arms, whacking the fat man in the back of the head, crosses his ankles, and bows. The man, meanwhile, has not stirred, has not even ceased his dark sullen stare. His bulbous nose seems to fill up his face with a kind of thickening gloom, under which his moustaches hang lifelessly as though from a gibbet. Uneasily, Charlie tucks the napkin back under the fat chin, pats it down. He slides the soup bowl nearer. The man stares past it. Charlie pushes the bowl back into the line of his stare and stands there scratching his curly head. He strolls past nonchalantly and bumps into him, breaks as though to run, stops, frowns. He prods him with his elbow. He snaps the man's heavy suspenders. He raps him on the head with his cane, turns and kicks him with the back of his heel. He cocks his fists like a boxer, circles the man, punching at him with light jabs. He pulls his fat nose. He assumes a fencer's stance and thrusts at him with his cane. Nothing. Charlie shrugs irritably, turns away, spies the custard pies cooling on the counter. His eyes light up. He hefts a couple, judging their weight and balance, chooses one, turns to throw it. The fat man is as before, slumped heavily at the table, glowering into his bowl of hot soup. Charlie sidles up to the table, shows the man the pie, imposing it between his face and the soup, then hurries back to the counter and winds up to throw it. The man stares sullenly at the soup. Charlie's shoulders sag, he lowers the pie. The sparkle is gone from his eyes. He shakes himself. He squares his shoulders, dances closer, raises the pie again. He hops about aggressively, making faces and brandishing the pie, but all to no avail. He bangs on the table. He kicks the man in the shins. He bares his teeth, closes his eyes, and slaps the pie into his face.

But when he opens his eyes he discovers, to his horror, that it is not the fat man he has struck, but the beautiful lady on the hallway landing. Her pale melancholy features are smeared with custard and pieces of pie are splattered over her long white gown. For a moment Charlie seems frozen with shock, his hands clutching his curly hair, his mouth agape, eyes popping with disbelief. Then he gives a little leap and goes dashing about frantically in search of something to use as a towel, discovers some heavy drapes on a window. He grabs up a handful and rushes back, reaches the drapes' length, and gets snapped backwards into a pratfall. He scrambles to his feet, tangled in drapes and pullcord. He lurches toward the lady, tears springing to his dark-lashed eyes, only to get jerked back again. The more he tries to free himself, the more entangled he becomes. The lady stands there by the balustrade, high above the checkerboard marble floor below, gazing off vacantly, wistfully, her face crusted with custard and pastry flakes. Bits slide slowly down her cheeks, dropping off her chin onto her bosom like melting candlewax. Charlie fights his way out of the curtains at last, dragging the pullcord with him. He unwinds himself from the cord in a speeded-up sequence of little twirls, leaps, and pas de chat, then bounds forward to wipe the lady's face, first with his hands, then his hat, the drapes, his jacket, his tie. She blinks inside all the paste, her lashes clotted with custard. He pulls out his shirttail, dabs gently at her eyes.

Which are not her eyes at all, but the old man's. Charlie is standing in the library, dabbing at the old man's rheumy eyes with his shirttail. The library is a shambles, the books spilled from their shelves, the paintings slashed and fallen, ashtrays tipped, vases and statuary smashed, glasses strewn, mirrors shattered, clocks split open, their works springing out like wild hairs. The old man is standing amid all this debris by his writing desk, tears running down his pale lined cheeks and into his white goatee, his top hat crushed, his hands in his pants. The ink bottle has been tipped over. The ink stands in a glossy black puddle, perfectly outlined against the desktop as though it might be made of rubber, like a child's practical joke. The old man, his goatee dripping with tears, gazes imploringly at Charlie, his hands moving funereally inside his black trousers. He wears a black armband, and his pince-nez dangles at his chest, the lenses fogged with a thousand tiny fractures. Charlie, dabbing still at the old man's eyes as though unable to stop himself, knocks one of the eyeballs loose. Slowly it oozes out of its socket, squirts free, and slides down his withered cheek, hanging there by a slippery thread. Desperately, Charlie tries to push the eyeball back in place, but it is difficult even to hang on to it: it keeps popping and slithering out of his grasp. And then the other one begins to ooze from its socket.

Charlie cries out and claps his hand against the extruding eye, only to find that what he has clapped is the maid's round white bottom. She is bent over, making up the crumpled bed, her bloomers around her ankles. Charlie recoils, staggering backwards, trips over his own cane, hooked in the bloomers, and tumbles into a stack of hatboxes. The maid peeks around at Charlie, past her radiant buttocks, then, reaching back and spreading her cheeks at him, purses her lips and blows him a kiss. He gasps, scrambles to his feet, wheels around and slaps up against the wall. He gropes his way in blind panic to a door, her bared behind flashing at him in a dozen mirrors, the walls turning soft as flesh. The air seems to be full of fluttering lingerie. He fumbles clumsily with the door handle, which keeps slipping out of his grasp as though greased, finally throws his shoulder against the door and crashes out of there.

Only to find himself back in the kitchen again. The large bald man, however, is no longer sitting at the table. His chair has fallen behind him as though kicked away, and he stands now, pissing sullenly into his soup bowl. Charlie picks himself up and, trembling, hunched over his bruised shoulder, backs away. He bumps up against a counter, puts his hand back to brace himself, plants it in a custard pie. The fat man buttons up and shuffles over to the door. He kneels, scowling darkly, and peers intently through the keyhole. His broad suspenders are stretched taut over his heavy body, the napkin dangling under his chin like a signal flag. Charlie, licking the pie from his hand, edges over toward the man. He tries to peek through the same keyhole, but the hole is too small and the fat man is immobile before it, utterly spellbound. Charlie pushes and shoves from all angles and finally, his ear pressed to the fat man's ear, gains a glimpse. What he sees throws him into a state of whey-faced alarm. He tries frantically to drag the door open, but the fat man is a dead weight before it. He kicks him, punches him, pulls him by the ears, smashes a chair over his head, but he cannot be budged. Charlie pounds his own head in despair, then pauses. A light seems to have dawned. He searches under his coat and shirttails, finds the large safety pin holding up his pants: he unfastens it, rams the point deep into the fat man's behind. Slowly, as though receiving a distant but utterly dismaying message, the fat man rears up, his mouth commencing gradually to gape, his face to twist and darken, his heavy moustaches to bristle, his eyes to gather focus. Charlie, holding up his unpinned pants, dashes past him out the door.

In the hallway on the stair landing, the lady in the white gown has fashioned a noose out of the pullcord Charlie dragged down from the drapes. She has tied the loose end around the broad railing of the balustrade and is fitting the noose itself around her neck. Her face is still smeared, her dress blotched, with custard cream pie. Charlie bounds toward her, holding up his baggy trousers with one hand, waving the other frantically, but the noose is already necklacing her pale throat. He pleads with her, he blusters, he cajoles, but the woman, leaning dangerously against the polished balustrade, gazes past him, down into the empty hallway. Charlie reaches toward her, but something in her dark clotted earnestness holds him back. He hops and dances around her, biting his nails, whimpering, his eyes filling with tears. He presses his palms together beseechingly, his pants fall down. He yanks them up, but sees that the woman has turned to look at him at last. Taking heart, he twirls his cane for her with one hand, then tries in vain to tip his hat and hold up his pants at the same time with the other. As he grabs for his pants, hat, pants, hat, her melancholy expression seems to soften. He prances around her in a frenzied teary-eyed imitation of glee, taking pratfalls, bumping his head, dropping his pants, losing his hat, attempting all the while to lure her away from the balustrade. She remains, leashed by the pullcord, but seems more and more caught up in his act. He juggles his hat and cane, plays peekaboo with her through a leafy potted plant, eats one of the leaves as though distracted by her beauty, executes a cartwheel without losing either hat or trou-

sers, fiddles a tune on a barometer snatched from the wall. The
woman wipes a blob of custard pie from her cheek as though
brushing away a tear, seems to have forgotten the rope around
her neck. Charlie, eyes darting about as though running out of
ideas, removes his hat to mop his brow, discovers an old cigarette
butt tucked inside the band. His face lights up. He puts the bent
butt in his mouth, pats his pockets for a match, holding his pants
up first with one hand, then the other. He shrugs, snaps his fingers, plucks an imaginary match out of the air, which he proceeds
to strike on his backside. He jumps up in the air as though having
set the seat of his pants on fire, then hops about fanning out the
flames. The woman clasps her hands together in front of her face,
peering at him over her fingertips. He struts up and down the
landing, puffing on the bent cigarette, blowing imaginary smoke
rings. He uses his vest pocket for an ashtray, stubs the butt out on
the sole of his shoe, loses it momentarily in the hole there, pretending to have given himself a hotfoot. He finds the butt again,
winks, flicks it over his shoulder, kicks it high with his heel,
catches it in his hat. The lady seems fascinated now and, though
she has still not smiled, watches him intently. Encouraged, Charlie plucks the butt out of the hat, holds it up before her, breaks it
in two pieces, hitches his pants high, pinching them in place with
his elbows, and flicks both bits of cigarette over his shoulders: he
leaps up with both feet and kicks the two halves in the air at the
same time, simultaneously dropping his pants. He catches one
piece in his hat, lurches, shackled by fallen trousers, for the
other, crashes into the young woman and knocks her over the balustrade. At first he cannot even grasp what has happened, spinning about frantically in search of the woman as though she might
have vanished into thin air. He peers fearfully over the railing and
discovers her there below, twisting and jerking at the end of the
pullcord, struggling in vain to free herself. Charlie, aghast, tries
to reach her, cannot, tries to pull her back up, lacks the strength.
He fumbles with the knot around the balustrade, but his hands are
shaking. He races down the stairs, tries to reach her from below,
but she is hanging several feet above him, her feet twitching,

kicking. He drags a chair over, leaps up on it, tries to hold her up by pushing on her feet, but her knees keep buckling. She kicks him in the ear, and knocks him off the chair. He scrambles to his feet, clutching his curly hair in anguish, spies the suit of armor. He tries to wrench away its halberd, but it seems permanently locked into the gauntlet. He cannot stop to consider alternatives: he hauls the whole apparatus, clashing and bouncing, up the stairs with him. He props the armor against the balustrade, takes a furious backswing with the halberd, and the suit of armor follows, crawling up his face and bowling him over. He struggles out from under, his face striped by cuts and scratches. He is no longer even trying to keep his trousers up, but neither does he have time to kick them off. He lifts the armor on his shoulders as though carrying a wounded warrior, takes another mighty backswing over the knotted pullcord, and the blade of the halberd flies off, disappearing through an open doorway. He dumps the armor off his back, grabs up his pants, and chases after it.

In the next room, however—the bedroom, as it turns out—the halberd blade is nowhere to be seen. He fumbles through perfume bottles, hatboxes, scattered clothing, finally turns to race out again without it, draws up short: the maid stands before the closed door, writhing provocatively, wearing nothing now but her bright white apron. She reaches beneath it and, pursing her lips, draws out the halberd blade, dripping with blood. Charlie gasps, whirls, and dashes pell-mell out another door.

He collides with a large leafy potted plant and goes sprawling across the brightly polished floor with its alternating black and white squares, slams into the stairway, and for a moment just lies there, holding his head. Then suddenly it all comes back to him—he starts up, looks one way, the other, straight ahead, up: the young woman in the white gown is directly above him, kicking feebly against her long skirts, her hands digging at the pullcord noose around her neck. Charlie jumps up and down, trying to run in all directions at once. He clambers up the balustrade, cannot reach her, jumps down, pushes a chair under the mounted deer's head, hops up and grabs the deer's nose, his pants falling around his ankles. He holds on with one hand while pulling his pants back up with the other, finally succeeds in throwing one leg over an antler and hauling himself up on the head. He stretches out toward the struggling woman, gives her a little push. She swings away from him, then back: he leans out and gives another push, harder than before. She swings further away, her skirts fluttering, her feet kicking, then back: he reaches out for her and at the same moment disappears from sight as the deer and antlers rip away from the wall and crash to the marble floor below. He disentangles himself from the wreckage. Soft shadows flicker back and forth across his terrified face, thrown by the swinging lady above him. He kicks the deer's head in bitter frustration, discovers the door behind it, gives it a try.

His face lights up when he finds himself in the bathroom. The policeman is in there, arms folded on his chest, standing near one end of the tub, which is now filling with water. Charlie grabs him, tries to drag him toward the hallway. The policeman, his helmet set square over his broad brow, his brass buttons polished and handlebar moustache neatly groomed, spreads his legs slightly, plants both fists on his hips, and squints down at Charlie, as though considering an arrest. Charlie is jumping up and down frantically, pointing at the door, mimicking a hanged man, begging the policeman to come with him. The policeman strokes his burly jaw thoughtfully, then squares his shoulders, slaps his billy-club in one big hand, and gazing past Charlie toward the challenge beyond the doorway, strides manfully forward. He steps on a bar of soap, his feet fly up in the air, and he falls—*splat!*—to his backside on the bathroom floor. He looks around in puzzlement, gets slowly to his feet, steps on the bar of soap, and falls—*splat!*—to his backside on the bathroom floor. He scowls, glances from side to side suspiciously, leaps quickly to his feet, steps on the bar of soap, and falls—*splat!*—to his backside on the bathroom floor. Charlie tries to help him up, but the policeman belts him with his billy, a blow that sends Charlie reeling and wheezing across the room. The policeman rises cautiously, steps on the soap, and falls—*splat!*—to his backside on the bathroom floor.

Charlie, still doubled over by the policeman's blow, is staggering back and forth from door to policeman to door to policeman, tearing out his hair and trying to keep his pants up. The policeman stands, steps on the soap, and falls—*splat!*—to his backside on the bathroom floor. Charlie is weeping, banging on the wall with his fist. The policeman is standing, slipping, falling—*splat! splat!*—over and over again. Charlie turns and stumbles despairingly out of the bathroom, face buried in his sleeve.

He trips over the crumpled suit of armor: he is back in the hallway but now up on the landing once more. He wipes away the tears, pulls up his pants, leans over the railing: whatever he might have hoped, she is still down there, hanging by her slender neck at the end of the pullcord, swaying gently from the push he has given her. Her hands, though fallen to her sides, continue to scratch weakly at the air. He tugs again on the cord, tries to bite through it with his teeth, saw it in two against the railing. All in vain. Her body, still twitching faintly in its long white gown, turns slowly round and round below him at the end of the rope, her eyes staring up at him in black anguish, her long flowing hair tangled and pasty with custard pie. Charlie beats his brow in dismay. The light dims as though she were spinning shadows with her feathery turnings. Her mouth opens slowly as if to speak, her swollen tongue emerging like a final stiff rebuke. Charlie gasps, yanks up his trousers, and plunges blindly through another door in search of something with which to cut the cord.

It is, though through a different door, the boudoir again. He starts to turn away, but then does a double take: over on the dressing table, among the vials and sprays and spilled jewelry boxes, there is, aglow as though spotlit, a pair of silver scissors! He rushes toward the table and the lights go out. When they come on again, he is sprawled on the floor near the table, one leg over a silk-cushioned chair, the thick carpet about him littered with shoes, perfume bottles, pale twists of flimsy underthings, glittering bits of broken glass. The scissors are gone. Across the room in front of a mirror, the maid is standing in her bloomers and apron, snipping the buttons off the front of her vest with the scis-

sors, then tossing them over her shoulder and kicking them high
in the air with the heel of her shoe. Charlie pulls himself painfully
to his feet and, in a rage, hurls himself at her, but even as he
plunges it is into darkness as again the lights go out, returning to
find him bang up against a wall, blood running from his nose into
his black moustache. The maid peeks coquettishly at him from
behind the bed, its canopies hanging obscurely now like weighted
webs, there and not there: it is as though there were a new distance between them, a graininess in the space that was not there
before. She pops out, legs spread, and, whipping her bodice open,
flashes her breasts at him. They glow in the gathering dimness as
though lit from within, pimpled by dark little nipples like pupils of
frightened cartoon eyes. Even as Charlie pushes away from the
wall, the lights blink off and on again. Though the maid is still
there in the same place, wearing only her apron like a frilly dinner
napkin, the bed is gone—in fact, the whole room is turned
around. Terrified, Charlie turns to flee—but no, it was a mirror
image: he crashes into her and they fall together onto the unmade
bed. He struggles to free himself but becomes entangled in the
bedclothes. He loses his derby. He burrows into the linens to recover the derby, loses his pants. He recovers his pants, loses a
shoe. He leaves it, staggering away toward the door, dragging the
canopy with him—but the maid blocks the way, squeezing her
bare breasts at him, swaying her white aproned hips, smirking
provocatively. He threatens her with his cane, but she only turns
her backside toward him in open invitation. He spins away toward
another door, but there she is, holding her apron out in front of
her, shaking it at him as though taunting a mad bull, the scissors
between her teeth like a rose. He backs away, tripping over the
debris on the carpet, bumping into things in the deepening haze.
Only she is bright, brighter than ever, her eyes sparkling, her
flesh glowing, the black shaggy patch of pubic hair winking at him
from behind the fluttering white apron like the negative of a sputtering lightbulb. His hand closes around a doorknob—he whips it
open and leaps through, but it is only a closet: he thumps up
against the wall, falls back in a thick bind of knotted gowns and

petticoats, straddled by the grinning maid. He clambers to his feet, losing his derby between her squeezing thighs, and tries to escape, but she backs him up against the wall and, standing on his trousers, rips his shorts away. He opens his mouth to cry out: she stuffs it full with one of her plump breasts, then, pushing his derby down around his ears, her knee jammed between his legs, commences to trim away his little moustache with the scissors. He closes his eyes, shudders: the maid slips and the scissors jab his nostrils. He gasps in pain and seems to get the maid's breast caught in his throat. He staggers about, gagging and snorting, crashing into things, taking pratfalls, dragging the startled maid with him. Tears are streaming down his puffed-out cheeks. The maid is pushing on his face, hanging on to his ears, prying at his jaws, her own mouth agape with torment and effort. At last the breast pops free and they fall apart, somersaulting away from one another as though spring-loaded. The maid, clutching her breast, crawls over by the dressing table, tears clouding her darkly lined eyes. Her belly has gone soft, the soles of her feet are dirty, her hair is snarled. She tosses him the scissors as though breaking an engagement, crawls under the table. He twitches what remains of his moustache, takes up the scissors, and, watching the maid warily, hitches up his pants and backs out of the room on his hands and knees. The maid seems to have shrunk. She is curled up under the dressing table, her thumb in her mouth, like a small tearful child, like the child perhaps of the faded photograph on the table above her, abandoned, some promise broken, in a studio boudoir festooned with rumpled clothing and jagged mirror fragments like sequins, its flowered wallpaper already starting to peel.

Charlie turns around and finds himself in the bathroom once more, one shoe off and one shoe on, gripping not a pair of scissors but a limp douche bag. The policeman, fully uniformed, is sitting in the bathtub, chest-high in water. His stern manly features are lined now with worry, his rugged jaw is grimly set, his eyes asquint. Charlie wipes his face with his sleeve and, still on his hands and knees, crawls over to plead with him once more, but the policeman ignores him, his gaze narrowed instead upon a small flock of rubber ducks floating between his legs. His uniform is black and ripply beneath the surface, the brass buttons appearing to float free. Water has crept up through the wool of his coat and laps darkly now at the edges of his untarnished badge. Suddenly his arm flashes out of the gray bathwater, his fist clutching a billyclub: he brings it down with all his might—*pow!*—on one of the rubber ducks. Water geysers out of the tub, splattering Charlie, the walls, the floor, even the overhead light bulb, making it fizzle and pop, but the duck bobs placidly back to the surface. Again and again the policeman smashes at the duck with his club, but always the duck bobs back. The policeman's shoulders slump, his arm goes slack. He looks up at Charlie. Water is dripping off the edge of his bell-like helmet, off his nose and the tips of his handlebar moustache. Charlie points to the door again, tears in his eyes, clutching the douche bag as though in offering, but receives only a blank stare in return. Then, slowly, the policeman begins to smile. The smile spreads, showing his teeth: the two in front are missing. Charlie blinks in disbelief. The policeman's eyes cross. He bobs his eyebrows, waggles his tongue. He snatches Charlie's douche bag away, peers inside, gives a squeeze: it is filled with ink which blackens the policeman's face. The tips of his moustache fly up, his helmet spins around, steam shoots out his ears. He bops Charlie on the head with his billy, bops himself on the helmet. Everything seems to be speeding up. Buttons fly off the policeman's coat like popping corn. He stretches his lower lip up over his nose, his badge shoots sparks, his ears flap. He gives Charlie his douche bag back, points him toward the door, bops him with the billy again. He gives himself another blow on the helmet and sinks into the water, his eyeballs—stark white now behind the black ink—rolling round and round, the rubber ducks bobbing.

Charlie creeps miserably away, holding the douche bag to his thumped head: the policeman has sent him into the kitchen where the large bald-headed man with the napkin under his chin is waiting for him. The man tears away the douche bag—no longer a douche bag, in fact, but somehow now a rabbit with its head cut

off—and swats him with the bloody end of it. The blow sends
Charlie tumbling head over heels into a sideboard stacked with
white dishes which come clattering down on him. Charlie struggles dizzily to his feet, his trousers binding his ankles, peers
around for his hat and takes another blow from the rabbit, a fero-
cious stroke across the shoulders that rockets him into the wood-
pile, sending the logs flying and splintering, bringing down fire
tools and pots and pans, cracking the tiles in the wall. The fire has
died down and shadows crowd up around him. Out of these shadows now rocks the fat man, swinging the beheaded rabbit menacingly by its hind paws. Charlie scrambles toward a table, but
before he can slip under it he is caught with a blow that whips him
upside down, a kick to the belly that doubles him up, another to
the face that arches him backward and sprinkles the tablecloth
with a spray of blood. The fat man yanks at the tablecloth, bringing everything on top of it down on Charlie: a buffeting avalanche
of plates and glasses, mashed potatoes, soup and custard pies,
knives, forks, and butter dishes, mustard pots, gravy bowls.
Charlie, his face puffing up, lies there in the garbage, almost unable to move. The fat man rises over him now like some bloated
colossus in shirtsleeves and suspenders, his bald head high above,
near the ceiling somewhere, lost in the shadows. The man rears
back and brings the headless rabbit down punishingly on Charlie,
pounding him again and again, up and down his ragged body,
Charlie rolling around in a syrupy tangle of trousers and tablecloth, soup, piss, and pies, unable even to defend himself now, the
blows raining down—not so much separate blows, as a single
blow repeated over and over as though on an endless loop: the
mighty backswing, the whipping downstroke, the bruising wallop
and splattering blood, each backswing a kind of reverse of the
downstroke, the rabbit seeming almost to suck back its own blood
on the upswing, replenishing itself as it were for the next blow,
Charlie jerking spasmodically from one side to the other as
though in the grip of a violent fit of hiccups, his own blood and
tears ebbing and flowing with each spasm, the debris around him
sliding back and forth as though choreographed. The only differ-

ence from one blow to the next is the increase of anguish in Charlie's eyes, the intensifying of terror. Slowly, even as the blows fall steadily, almost mechanically, small changes begin to occur: One of Charlie's arms pushes sluggishly out of the pattern. His body gradually rotates until he is on his side, on his belly, on his hands and knees, struggling upwards. One foot strains forward under his body, knocks a dancing fork askew. The fat man's strokes continue as before—up, back, forward, down, up, back, forward, down—but Charlie, as though clawing his way through an atmosphere as thick as custard pie, is gradually dragging himself out from under, gaining an inch here, reaching out two inches there, slowly picking up momentum, until at last he is able to wrench free, snatch up his pants, and hurl himself through the kitchen door.

He lies there for a while in the next room, choking and wheezing, his battered limbs awry. The room is dark, lit only by a few distant candles, but he can see that he is back in the library again. It is immaculate, everything in it—everything except himself—restored to its former condition. The books are in their shelves, the paintings back up on the walls, the mirrors whole and ashtrays upright, the Oriental carpets unlittered. Even the clocks are all working again, the old grandfather clock's brass pendulum flashing rhythmic pinprick signals as it reflects in its steady swing the soft flickering glow of the candles. The candles surround a closed coffin. Agleam with high polish and candlelight, it is the only object clearly visible in the darkened room. Beyond it: a faint thin fog of gray light from a far door ajar. Charlie, unable to stand, drags himself toward that door across the tightly woven carpets, but as he nears the coffin, he freezes, his bloodied mouth agape: *the lid is opening!* Just a crack at first, a quivering suggestion merely of something about to happen, but slowly the crack widens, releasing the blackness within, a kind of pool of absolute darkness leaking out, making the candles dip and gutter—and then a hand: white, gnarled, emaciated, tremulously pressing the lid back. Just that hand, and the blackness, and the rising lid. Charlie watches, stupefied, as the head emerges, weaving unsteadily as if unhinged. It is the old man's head with its white goatee, wearing its top hat still and its gleaming pince-nez, but greatly shrunken, white as chalk, and with empty shadowy craters where its eyes should be. The head swivels stiffly as though trying to locate itself, the lips drawn back in a rigid grin, exposing the spiky teeth—then suddenly the hand loses its grip: the lid comes crashing down, severing the head from its neck. The head drops to the carpet. There is a dim candlelit pause. Charlie holds his breath. Then, once more, the lid begins to open. Again there is a leakage of blackness from within, again the appearance of a pale shriveled hand. Again the candles flare and dip. This time the lid opens all the way back, spilling flowers and dousing candles in the final clumsy arc of its fall. The headless body of the old man rises from the casket in its formal black suit. It moves stiffly, ceremoniously, lifting one limb out and then another. It lowers its feet to the floor, stands rigidly free from the casket, tipping from side to side. It reaches out blindly, lifts its foot, steps on its own grinning head: the head rolls, the body's feet fly up in the air, and it falls—*splat!*—on its backside on the Oriental carpet. Charlie, eyes squeezed shut, arms and legs churning, reaches the half-open door and, without looking back, pitches on through.

He is back where he began. But the checkered marble floor where he lies is dulled now with dust, the hallway itself suffused in a granular, almost unearthly, pallor. The mirrors reflect nothing, there is no sheen on the broad balustrade, and spiderwebs now loop and raddle from the chandelier, the staircase and potted plants, the hanging lady. He peers up at her through swollen eyes. She dangles limply from the pullcord noose, inert and wizened, though still disquietingly beautiful, wrapped in long tangled skeins of hair and the lacy moth-eaten gown. Has so much time passed? Charlie shudders. He grips the doorframe, pulls himself to his feet, then shuffles, shackled by his fallen trousers, to a table in one corner, taking loose swinging swipes as he goes at the dusky nets of web and dust. With great effort, he drags the table out of the corner, pushes it under the woman. He leans wearily against the table a moment, looking around, spies a chair tipped over near the fallen deer's head, the head mossy now, its glass eyes furred with dust, its antlers enmeshed in cat's cradles of ropy webs and dried rose stems. He hauls the chair out of the debris, stirring puffs of coiling dust, sets it on the table. Then he pulls up his baggy trousers, crawls up onto the table himself, steadies the chair, mounts it. He can reach the lady now, but not the noose. He sighs, steps down again, his movements sluggish and ungainly. He finds a plant stand large enough to hold the chair, dumps the dead plant to the floor, sets the stand on the table. He climbs up, lifts the chair onto the plant stand. But there is not enough room for him now on the plant stand, so he lowers the chair to the table, crawls up on the plant stand, brings the chair up after him. The light in the hallway has been fading, as though losing itself in the dust and webs: it is hard now to see more than a few feet away. Even as he clambers up on the plant stand, the table is disappearing into the gathering dimness below. He hesitates, weaving dizzily, but braces himself, sets the chair on the stand between his legs, and crawls up on it, the whole apparatus rocking dangerously with each movement. He kneels up there for a moment, unable even to open his eyes. Then he does open them and, gazing fixedly at the hanging lady, rises totteringly to his feet. He reaches for the noose. A chair leg wobbles to the edge of the plant stand, tips over. Charlie grabs the woman, his pants falling to his ankles. The chair falls away into nothingness, the plant stand following after. The lady's dress gives way: Charlie slips to her waist; reflexively, he locks his knees around her as well. He can see nothing below him—nor above him: the balustrade too has vanished into the deepening shadows, the darkness irising in on him like the onset of blindness. He can see only the hanging lady whose ravaged white gown in his desperate grasp is flaking away like pie crust and whose neck is stretching in its noose like stiff taffy. He clings to her, pants adroop, tears in his eyes, shadows creeping over his face like bruises, gazing out into the encircling gloom with a look of anguish and bewilderment, as though to ask: What kind of place is this? Who took the light away? And why is everybody laughing?

One Moment While the Operator Changes Reels

INTERMISSION

The lights come up and a thin curtain covers the screen, but the sign behind it telling everyone to please visit the concession stands in the lobby while they're getting ready for the next feature can still be seen, and the ripply picture on it of a huge drippy banana split, which they don't even sell as far as she knows, makes her stomach rumble loud enough to give a zombie hiccups, so she decides to go out and see what she can find with less than six zillion calories in it. Her friend, who's flirting with some broken-nosed character a row back in a high school letter jacket and sweaty cowboy hat, turns and asks her jokingly to bring her back a salty dog—"Straight up, mind!"—making the guy snort and heehaw and push his hands in his pockets.

In the lobby, there's a line for everything—candy, soft drinks, popcorn, cigarettes, ice cream, even the water fountain. The soft drinks line is the shortest so she gets in it, though the smells of minty chewing gum, chocolate, and hot butter are driving her crazy. She feels like she's caught in that Chinese torture movie where they locked this guy in a steel collar with his arms tied be-

hind him and left his food two inches from his mouth until he finally strangled himself to death trying to get at it. Her unhappy
tum complains again and she grabs a fistful and squeezes it just to
remind herself why she's being so mean to it.

At almost the same moment, some creep behind her, as though
to say and that ain't all, kid, grabs a handful of what her girlfriend
calls her holey altar—"You just kneel down and kiss it, honey!"
she likes to say—numb from so much sitting, but not so numb she
doesn't go lurching into the smart-alecky young schoolkids in
front of her, setting off a lot of sniggering insults, mostly about
her bosom, which is among more adult audiences usually her best
feature. She turns to scowl at the masher behind her, but there's
no one there. Instead, over by a movie poster advertising a sexy
religious epic, there's this dazzling guy, all class and muscle, a
real dreamboat, as they used to say in her favorite musicals, looking somehow heroic and vulnerable at the same time, and dressed
in clothes they don't even sell in a town like this—and he's staring straight at her! She's almost sure she recognizes him from
somewhere, not from this dump of course, it would have to be
from some movie—like possibly he was a private eye with a tragic
past or a great explorer or an alcoholic or a happy-go-lucky guy
who gave his life for the woman he loved, something like that.
Maybe even a half-naked martyr from that religious opus behind
him, a show, if so, she wouldn't want to miss, much as she
admires his present wardrobe. She sucks in her tummy and
takes a breath to lift her breasts a tad, just in case he might be
interested (fat chance, she cautions herself, all too often a fool for
love, she's famous for it)—and amazingly enough, he *is!* He fits a
cigarette between his lips, curls his hands around it and lights it,
never once taking his eyes off her, glancing appreciatively down
at her breasts (her sudden gasp makes them quiver in her bra
cups like sing-along bouncing balls, she can tell by the way his
brows bob), then back up at her eyes once more. He smiles
faintly, blows smoke, then holds up the pack as though offering
her one.

When she walks over toward him, her heart's beating so hard
she's sure it must be showing through her blouse like she's got

something alive in there trying to get out, and she knows just what they've always meant when they say in the movies, "I felt like I was walking on air." Only it's a kind of bumpy air, like any minute something might catch her heels and make her fall on her face and turn the whole thing into some awful slapstick routine, the story of her crummy life. And sure enough, just when she gets close enough to pick up his smell (which is something between pepper steak, hot bathwater, and a Christmas tree—buttered popcorn can't touch it), her knees go all mushy, and she thinks, wobbling, oh boy, here we go again—but he reaches out and steadies her with just the lightest touch on her elbow, and then, as though there's some secret signal between them, they turn and (she checks to make sure she's still got her ticket stub, you never know, don't burn your britches, as her girlfriend likes to say) step out onto the street.

Her hands are trembling when she reaches for the cigarette he offers her, and there's a kind of fog swirling around (it makes her think of steamy train stations and damp farewells, though in fact she hasn't even said hello yet) or else she's going blind with mad passion, very likely, and she's just trying to think of something brainy yet romantic to say—like, "Isn't destiny wonderful, I agree, but it's sometimes, you know, kind of weird, too, am I right?" or, "When you looked at me in there, I felt like I was stumbling on air, me and my big feet," or maybe just, "How did you guess, yum, my favorite flavor," wondering to tell the truth what kinds of cigarettes they sold nowadays, not having tried to smoke one of the things since way back before she became a cheerleader her third year in high school—when four guys step out of the shadows and grab her and start dragging her toward the curb. "Hey!" she yelps, any language fancier than that escaping her as her feet leave the ground. She twists around toward her erstwhile lover-boy, hoping, if not for a heroic rescue, at least for a little sympathy, but he only smiles mysteriously, takes a drag on his butt, flips it away, and, trailing wisps of fog and cigarette smoke like a kind of end-of-reel tease, disappears back into the movie house.

A black unmarked car with thick windows pulls up and they

push her into it, two of these blue-suited meatsacks squeezing in beside her in the back seat, another jumping up front with the driver, who is hunched over the wheel in a cloth cap and a coat with the collar turned up around his ears, like something she has seen a thousand times, yet never seen before. The fourth guy flops a jump seat down in front of her and sits facing her with a machine gun pointed straight at her belly, which even in her present panic she realizes is what has gotten her into all this trouble in the first place. Maybe he can even hear it growling because, as they roar away from the curb, he tells her to shut up even though she hasn't said a word and couldn't if she tried.

It's scary enough that she's jammed into this car with a bunch of muscle-bound maniacs who, if they aren't gangsters, sure act like it, a gun poked at her stomach and the car going about a hundred miles an hour through the thickest downtown traffic she's ever seen around this place, running lights and swerving around oncoming cars and generally scaring the pants off anybody who has time to see them coming (someone who looked a little bit like her mother just went leaping backwards through a plate glass window back there—this is no joke!), but she's also got the distinct impression that the driver, who should have his eyes on the road ("Yikes!" she yips as the side of a huge bus looms before them and the guy with the gun gives her a jab with it and says: "I thought I told you to shut up!"), has them on her instead, staring darkly at her through his rearview mirror, like either he's got designs on her, evil or whatever, or he's trying to tell her something. "There's somebody followin' us," he snarls suddenly, as though to hide what he really wants to say.

The other guys whip out their weapons and roll the windows down. *"Step on it!"* the one with the gun on her yells and now they *really* get going, jumping curbs and racing the wrong way down one-way streets, taking corners on two wheels, tires screeching, crashing right through newsstands and flower carts, beating speeding engines to train crossings, leaping roadworks and gaping bridges, the gorillas beside her meanwhile leaning out the windows and blasting away at whoever it is that's following them. No one's paying any attention to her now, if they weren't going a thousand miles an hour she could just open the door and step out and never be missed—no one, that is, except the driver, who is still eyeing her through the rearview mirror like he can't get enough of her. Is he crazy?

Then suddenly one of the bruisers beside her slumps to the floor with a big hole where an eye should be, making her clench her teeth and pull her lips back, and the guy in the jump seat, looking like somebody just yanked his plug and let all the blood run out, shoves her toward the empty window and yells in a high nervous voice: "You think it's funny? You just stick *your* head out there for a while!" She shrinks back at the same moment that the gunman on the other side of her spasms and flops against her like a bag of dirty laundry (and where *are* they now? they seem to be racing along the edge of some *cliff!*), and she tries her best to erase the grimace, but the squeaky guy just screams and pokes her with his machine gun again. His finger is jittery on the trigger, his eyes rolling around like he's about to lose his taffy, and the driver, squinting at her in the mirror, gives her a little go-ahead nod as if he might have something in mind, so what else can she do?

They're going so fast her eyes tear when she sticks her head out and she can't see a thing, but she can hear the squealing tires and howling sirens and the bullets ricocheting off the side of the car. As for those two hours in the beauty parlor this afternoon, forget it, it's a good thing it's her own hair or it'd all be gone by now. Whenever she tries to pull back inside, she can feel that fruitcake behind her prodding at her fundamentals with the pointy end of his tommy gun, pushing her further and further out the window like he might be trying to unload ballast, as her girlfriend likes to say when she has to go to the ladies'. Then amazingly, amid the roar of rushing wind and gunfire and speeding wheels, she seems to hear someone whisper, *"Jump!"* right in her ear. What? She catches just a glimpse through her windblown lashes (*those* aren't her own, and—*zip!*—they're gone) of the brim of his cloth cap, leaning out the window toward her. *"Now!"*

The car seems to swerve and the next thing she knows she's all alone out in midair some place (out of the corner of her eye she sees the gangsters' car leave the cliff edge and go somersaulting explosively far below), and then she's falling. She doesn't know how long she keeps falling, maybe she passes out for a second, because it seems like almost the next day when she hits the water—which is cold as ice and churning like an old washing machine and wakes her up right away if in fact she was asleep before. She flounders in the swirling waves, wishing now she hadn't always been so self-conscious in a swimming suit and had at least gone to the pool enough to learn something about how you stay on top of this stuff and keep from swallowing so much of it. What's worse, when for a moment she does manage to get her head above the surface, she can see she's being swept toward some kind of rapidly approaching horizon, which even she in her landlocked innocence knows can only be the edge of a waterfall: the roar is deafening and she can see spume rising from below like the mist they use in those films about dying and going to the other world. Well, out of the frying pan and down the drain, as her friend would say: she holds her nose and gets ready for the plunge.

But, just as the current starts to pick up speed and propel her over the edge, along comes this empty barrel, tumbling and rolling in the waves, and sort of scoops her up, head first—and there she is, halfway inside, her head banging around on the bottom, her backside up in the air and feet kicking, when she feels the whole apparatus tip, pause, and then drop. It is not a pleasant ride. The half of her left outside feels very airy and vulnerable the whole way down, not unlike the way it felt when she got sent to the principal's office for a paddling in the fourth grade, while the half on the inside gets shaken around like the churning balls in a lucky numbers barrel. *Ow!* It hurts worse than the time she went rollerskating and got thrown off the tail end of a snakeline. Or the night her friends shoved some cotton candy and a double-dip ice-cream cone in her two hands and pushed her down the collapsing ramp of a carnival fun house, with a thousand people standing out front watching and laughing their fat heads off.

It seems to take centuries to get to the bottom, that's how it is when you think each second is going to be your last, but finally the whirling and pounding is over and she finds herself dizzily afloat, her head at the dark smelly end of the barrel, her legs dangling in the water, which does not seem so cold now. She knows the barrel's starting to fill up and sink, she has to do something soon, but her head hurts too much to think, and besides, it feels good just lying there like in a bathtub, all alone, the cool water swirling gently around her as though to kiss away the hurt. She remembers a movie she saw once in which this queen was taking her bubble bath when some gorgeous guy she'd never seen before came running in, being chased by the heavies and desperately needing some place to hide, so she gave him a kind of regal smile and let him duck into her bathwater. You couldn't see anything, the only way you could tell what was going on down there while the yoyos after him were clanking around grumpily stabbing at the curtains was by the majestic expression on the queen's face as she clawed at the edge of the tub. Just thinking about that movie makes her head hurt a little less.

A kind of chilly current passes under her and something tickles her thighs, giving her the shivers, so, somewhat reluctantly, she slides out of the barrel at last and, holding on to its rim, gazes dreamily around her. She seems to have been cast far out to sea: nothing but water in all directions. And then she sees them: fins slicing through the water! Sharks! *Hundreds* of them! She scrambles back into the barrel, kicking frantically, and by throwing her weight at the bottom tips it upright, even as those huge slimy things come streaking by, whumping and thumping against it, as though trying to tip it over again.

She squats down, peering over the edge at them, her heart in her throat (why is everything in this world so *hungry* all the time?), safe for the moment, but not for long: the barrel is more than half full of water, it's nearly up to her nibbles, as her girlfriend would say, and more is lapping in over the rim every minute. She tries to scoop it out with her hands, but it's too slow. Her shoe doesn't work much better. She makes a kind of bag out of her blouse, but it's too torn up to hold anything. She feels like she's in one of those slow-motion sequences in which the more you run the more you don't go anywhere. Finally what works best is her bra, always the friend closest to her heart, as the ads say. She develops a kind of fast jack-in-the-box motion, collapsing her hands together underwater, filling both cups at once, then quickly spreading them apart as she snaps the bra upward—splush! *whoosh!* splush! *whoosh!*—over and over again, like she might be trying to fill up the ocean.

Eventually the bra snaps—that much action it was never made for—but she has won the battle. She bails the rest out with her one remaining shoe. She notices the sharks have gone. Probably it just got too weird for them. Not that her problems are over of course. She's adrift in a leaky barrel on an endless ocean, no food, no water, not even a cough drop. Boy, isn't that the way it always is? The one time she's worked off enough calories to really let herself go, and they take away the concessions. She pulls what's left of her blouse back on, loosens the buttons at the waist of her skirt, and slumps once again into a cramped-up squat at the puddly bottom of the barrel, feeling empty and bloated at the same time. She'd chew on the ticket stub she's still clinging to if it weren't all soggy with sea brine.

Days pass; weeks maybe, she loses count. She gets lonely, exhilarated, depressed, raving mad, horny. Then one day, on the distant horizon, she sees smoke. Right away, of course, she thinks of somebody roasting hotdogs or marshmallows and starts paddling frantically toward it with her bare hands. This is not very effective. She makes a sail out of her skirt and holds it up between her arms, which works better. The smoke, she sees, is coming out of the top of a mountain. It's all a lot farther away than she'd thought. The sharks come back and she has to beat them off with her shoe, temporarily losing the use of her masts, as they might be called, but still, slowly, progress is made.

As she bobs, at last, toward the shore, her arms feeling like they're about twenty feet long and made of waterlogged lead, she sees that a welcoming party—a bunch of natives with long spears and flowery necklaces—has come out to meet her. Her skirt has shrunk so much she can't get it up past her knees, but her underpants have little purple and green hearts on them (ever a wishful thinker) and might easily be mistaken for a swimsuit, especially by foreigners who aren't wearing all that much themselves. She's not sure what you say to natives on occasions like this, but finally decides the best thing is just to wave and say hi. This doesn't work as well as she might have hoped. They grab her, tie her hands and feet to long poles, and start lugging her on their shoulders up the mountainside. "Volcano god much hungry," one of them explains, stroking his belly, and it's true she can hear its insides rumbling even worse than her own. "But, hey, I haven't eaten for weeks; shouldn't you at least fatten me up first?" she shouts back hopefully as he walks on ahead, but he doesn't hear her, or pretends not to.

At the lip of the volcano, just as they're about to heave her in—she can already feel the heat on her backside, smell the sulphur coiling around, it's a desperate situation, but what more can she do? she's never been good at languages—an argument breaks out. There's some little fellow there, who looks a lot like the driver of the gangsters' car but now with burnt cork smeared on his face, leaping about hysterically and screaming something about "Medicine man! Medicine man!" This sets off a lot of squawking and hallooing and spear rattling, but at last they untie her and send her off down the mountainside with kicks and spearswats, snatching up her rescuer and tossing him in instead. She can hear his fading yell for what seems like hours as she runs away down the trail they've sent her.

The trail leads to a small hut in a clearing, where a man stands waiting for her. It's the same guy she saw in the theater lobby, except his chest is bare and bronzed now and his shorts are so thin you can almost see through them. "The plan worked!" he exclaims, taking her in his arms. "We're alone at last!" Listen, there were probably easier ways, she might have said if she weren't so out of breath, but by now he is peeling back her blouse shreds and gazing pop-eyed at her best act, so what the heck. Don't step on them, as her friend would say.

He fills his hands with them, rolling them round and round, pinching the nipples between his fingers, having all kinds of fun, then leans down to give them a little lick with his tongue, which might be a lot more exciting if it didn't remind her how ravenous she is. That shoulder under her nose is about the most delicious thing she's seen since the invention of peanut butter. He gapes his mouth and is just about to take one of them in whole, when everything gets shaken by a tremendous explosion and suddenly a bunch of trees that were there aren't there anymore. He looks up anxiously, holding her close, and then another one whistles and hits, knocking them off their feet. *"Invasion!"* he cries and grabs her hand, dragging her, both of them scrambling on all fours, toward the jungle cover.

His hut gets hit next and it sends plumes of flame soaring miles into sky, debris bombing out everywhere: they've gotten away from it in the nick of time! What was he doing, running a dynamite factory in there? "My precious experiments!" he explains, gasping, as he pulls her, his pained face scratched and soot-streaked, on into the jungle. He leads her along a treacherous path through snarling panthers, shrieking birds, swamps full of crocodiles and mosquitos, until they reach a row of bunkers down near the beach, where a handful of exhausted soldiers are holding out against wave after wave of enemy invaders. He dumps a couple of bodies aside, grabs up their rifles, hands her one, and throws himself down into the bunker just as a dozen bullets ricochet off the lip of it. He pops up, guns down four or five invaders, ducks down again, the bullets pinging and whizzing around his ears, jeepers, he's something amazing. I'm in love! she thinks, unable to deny it any longer. I'm cuckoo, I'm on fire, I'm over the harvest moon! *"Get down!"* he yells at her. Oh yeah, right. Cripes! she's almost too excited to think straight!

She knuckles down beside him and he shows her how to use the rifle. He's such a cutiepie, she wishes he'd take another quick lap at what her friend calls her honey-dewzies, dangling ripely in front of him—or at anything else for that matter, she's open to suggestions—but, no, he's too busy jumping up and shooting at these other bozos, it's like some kind of obsession with him. Well, she'll try anything once, in spite of all the trouble that dubious principle has got her into in the past, she must be a slow learner. She picks out a gangly guy just splashing in at the shoreline, shooting dopily in all directions, gets him in her sights, and jerks the trigger. Wow, it nearly takes her arm right off at the shoulder! But it's fun watching him go down: he kind of spread-eagles and goes up in the air about six inches, falling flat on his back in the wave rolling in. She braces herself and takes another shot: it doesn't hurt as much as before, and this time the enemy soldier does a kind of pirouette, spinning on one foot and bouncing a little before flopping to the beach. She pops one in the face, propelling him into a backwards somersault, hits another in the knees and then in his cowlick when his hat comes off as he crumples toward her, gets this one in the belly button (misery loves company, she thinks, suffering an evil burbling and gargling behind her own) and that one in the ear, spins them around and doubles them over with shots in their ribs and finishes them off with bullets up their booboos, lines them up in her sights and blasts them two, three at a time, aims down their own barrels so their guns blow up in their faces. This is great! She never knew guys had so much fun!

But it's too good to last, as she might have known. She feels a tugging on the seat of her drawers and looks down: it's the sport she came with, lying wounded at her feet, a bloody bandage around his head, hands still clenching his smoking rifle, the knuckles raw, his eyes red with pain and fever. He seems to be trying to whisper something. She leans close. She can hear the enemy whooping and squealing as they scramble impetuously up the hill toward them like little kids on an Easter egg hunt. "There aren't many of us left!" he gasps. "You've got to go for help!" She starts to protest—where's the kick in that?—but he cuts her off with a sad endearing smile: "We're depending on you, sweetheart!" he wheezes, giving her a weak slap on her fanny like one pal to another, so what can she do?

She hurries back through the jungle, knocking off crocs and tigers as she goes, having pretty much got the hang of this shooting thing, but somehow, maybe because she can't get her lover off her mind (she thinks of him now as her lover, such intimacies as they've shared being no big deal for some people maybe, naming no names, but all histories, like they say, are relative), she takes a wrong turn and ends up in the desert. She tries to circle back round to the jungle, which she can still see on the horizon, but after plowing up and down a couple of dunes in her bare feet, she can't see it anymore, just acres and acres of endless sand. She tries to trace her footprints backwards, but after five or six steps, they disappear.

She thinks maybe it's about time to sit down and have a good cry, but while she's still only thinking about it, some guys in turbans, pajamas, and silky boots with curled toes come galloping along and snatch her up. "Hey, fellas, you wouldn't happen to have a cracker or something?" she asks hopefully, but they only heave her over the back end of the horse, her little hearts aloft, and go thundering off to some sheik's palace in an oasis.

So, okay, she's had a few surprises since the night she stepped into that movie lobby back in her old hometown all those years ago, but the biggest one is yet to come. This sheik is the very same guy who was standing under the poster and who she just left battling impossible odds back in that bunker, only now here he is with what is obviously a very phony moustache pasted on his lip, and she's made to understand that she's his new favorite and is to be his bride. Tonight. Of course, there are a lot of brides, the palace is full of veiled ladies sneaking about, there's a couple of dozen of them here in his bedroom alone, but she considers herself a gregarious person and doesn't mind company. She winks at the sheik to let him know she's in on whatever he's got in mind, but he only scowls darkly and bellows something about "stinking pig" and "prepare her for bridal sacrament." Okay, let him play it his way.

She's handed over to some eunuchs and serving girls who lead her down to a kind of shallow swimming pool full of bareass ladies and peel her rags off her. She pats her belly and points into her open mouth with her bunched fingers, but they don't get it. Oh well, it's a wedding, isn't it, probably there's going to be a banquet, she tells herself, ever the cheery optimist. She's just got her toe in the water, testing how hot it is, when up comes that driver of the gangsters' car again. The last couple of times she's seen him, he was crashing down a cliff in an exploding car and getting thrown into the maw of a smoking volcano, yet here he is again, disguised this time as a naked eunuch, and insisting to everybody that before her bath she has to be taken down to what he calls the "virginorium" for a health check.

Before she or anyone else can protest, he is hauling her at full pelt down a mirrored hall, her bare feet slapping boisterously on the marble floor, the rest of her all aquiver and goose-bumpy and no doubt rosy pink under all the grime. Her birthday suit, unfortunately, even as starved as she is, could still use a few tucks here and there, a fact that has probably not escaped all the people who are turning to stare at her galumphing by. He pushes her ahead of him suddenly into a dark corridor, presses his back to the wall, cranes his head around the corner. "It's clear!" he hisses. "There's a plane waiting out behind the camel barns. We've got to move fast!" "Wait a minute," she pants, "I know this guy, it's all right." "No, you don't! It's not who you think it is! This is his evil twin brother! Didn't you notice the telltale scar, the missing birthmark? Through forged papers he has stolen his brother's rightful inheritance! He'll stop at nothing! That's why you're involved!" "What?" It's getting pretty complicated. "Look, I'm not particular, they're both pretty cute." He seizes her wrist. "Let me show you something."

He drags her down more corridors, more stairs, more narrow passages. "Talk about stopping at nothing," she grumbles. They're now deep in the labyrinth of the palace. He puts his fingers to his lips, sidles cautiously toward a locked door. "This is the room of the favorites," he whispers. "First they dance for the sheik, they become his bride, and then they come here." He picks the lock with a piece of wire concealed mysteriously on his person. Inside: a whole roomful of severed heads! She screams. It's a kind of reflex. "I'm sorry, I don't know what came over me," she whispers. They can hear footsteps approaching. He strokes the stone wall like a blind man trying to guess what it is. Suddenly, just as the footsteps come clattering down the stairs into the corridor, a piece of the wall slides open and they slip behind it, pressing the wall quickly together again like completing a puzzle.

The secret passage leads back to the harem pool. "Grab your clothes and let's get out of here!" he rasps. It's hardly worth it, all that's left are her raggedy blouse and bikini pants, and it's a hot climate anyway, but she does as she's told, having always been an easygoing sort. While she's pulling them on, the other eunuchs and serving girls crowd around, trying to herd her back into the pool again, but her friend makes a slicing gesture at his throat and grabs her by the hair. They all understand this and back away. If they're so good at sign language, she wonders, why didn't they get her something to eat when she asked them? It's only slowly dawning on her just how sinister this place really is. He drags her away by the hair, which she thinks is pushing the realism a bit too far, but before she can complain, they run into some of the apes who kidnapped her in the first place.

The head-chopping act doesn't work with these guys. "You! Dance!" one of them grunts, pushing her brusquely toward the sheik's bedroom. She trips and falls. If she can't even walk, do these mugs think she can dance? Her eunuch chum helps her to her feet, whispering furtively in her ear, "All right, this is it, kid!" "But I'm a rotten dancer!" she whimpers. "All I can do is polka!" "All you gotta do is be yourself—believe me, you can do it! Now, get in there and show 'em your stuff! I'll be waiting at the plane!"

She gets shoved into the sheik's bedroom where there's a big crowd gathered for her show, and the sheik asks her in his clumsy unpleasant accent, which she still suspects must be some kind of put-on, why she hasn't got out of her dirty old rags ("feelty olt wrecks," he calls them), and, thinking fast, she tells him that what she'd planned to do as her first number is the "Dance of the Filthy Pig." He looks skeptical and she tells him that it's very popular right now where she comes from and just to sit back and have a good time. She's never danced alone in public before, but once she's thought up the title, the rest comes easy. Anyone can do a dancing pig, especially if they've had a little cheerleading practice. She throws in a bit of dancing duck and dancing cow, which has the sheik boggling his eyes and twisting the ends of his moustache, and she might have gone on and done the whole barnyard (already—she can't help herself—she's thinking career) if they hadn't interrupted her with a loud gong and presented her with a covered platter: a banquet, after all! Her stomach gurgles shamelessly in anticipation.

What she finds when she lifts the lid, however, is the severed head of her eunuch friend, now wearing his old cloth driving cap, something metal between his pale blue lips. A key! She's crying on the inside, or maybe even throwing up, but on the outside she laughs crazily and snatches up the cloth cap with one hand, subtly cops the key with the other: bless his heart, his jaws are clamped around the key and she has to push on his face to get it out, sending the head rolling around on the marble floor, but this only adds authenticity to her second rendition, which she has just announced as "Follow the Bouncing Head." She tugs the cap down tight over her eyebrows and starts dancing wildly around the room, kicking the head ahead of her and chasing after, and, before they can recover from their amazement, boots it out the door and down the hall.

By the time she's found a way out of this pretzely loonybin, she can hear them clattering and shouting right behind her. This is going to be close! She sends her friend back down the corridor on one last mission, hoping to bowl a few of them over, and races out into the moonlight. She has no idea where the camel barns might be, but she just follows her nose and finds them soon enough. She lets the camels loose to confuse her pursuers, but the stupid things just stand there, chewing their cuds. "Next time I'm going to do the 'Dance of the Camelburgers'!" she screams furiously at them, and dashes out back where the old museum-piece of an airplane is parked. Even as she jumps up into the cockpit, she can hear the barns filling up behind her with rabid scimitar-swinging soreheads.

Her hands are trembling as she tries to figure out where to put the key in (she can just hear her girlfriend saying, "Honey, put it anywhere it feels good!"), and she realizes, as though it's just dawning on her, that she hasn't got the dimmest notion how to fly one of these clunkers. She doesn't even know how to drive a car, and on bicycles she's the town joke. Even walking is not easy for her. Still, those head-hunting goons are already clambering up on the wing with blood in their eyes, so what choice has she got? When she finally does locate the slot, everything happens violently at once: she's suddenly gunning madly down the field at full throttle, bouncing and careening, shedding startled assassins, probably there's a clutch or something she should have used, but too late now, all that's ancient history, right now she's got only one problem and that's how to get this gazunkas up in the air before she hits something—like those camel barns, for example, coming straight at her. She seems to have got spun around, and all those guys in the pajamas who were chasing her have stopped in their tracks, gaped a moment in wild-eyed shock, and are now racing each other for the barns once more.

She pulls, punches, twists, kicks, flicks, slaps, and screams at every doobob on the panel in front of her, but nothing works, so she finally just closes her eyes, hugs the steering gidget between her legs (maybe she's thinking about one of the old chewed-up dolls she still sleeps with on lonely nights, which is to say, most all the time, or else maybe that scrawny ginger cat she used to have, may he rest in peace), and shrinks back from the impending blow. Which doesn't come. She opens her eyes to find the old clatter-trap miraculously rattling straight up into the moonlit sky, the palace and then the oasis itself disappearing into the darkness behind her. Startled, she pushes the control stick away and— woops!—she's diving straight back to where she came from! All right, she's not completely stupid, a little pushing and pulling on that gizmo, and pretty soon the rollercoaster flattens out to something more like a horse race with hurdles.

Not bad for a jellybean, as her friend would say; in fact she'd be pretty proud of flying this contraption, first time like this, and by the seat of her pants as it were, if, one, that seat weren't so wet (listen, it was pretty *scary* back there for a while—who knows if all those terrorized movie heroines do any better, they don't show you *every*thing), and, two, there were some way of parking it and getting out without having to go all the way back down to the ground again. She pokes around for instructions, or even a bag of peanuts to calm her nerves, and comes on a sort of clockface on the panel in front of her with the minute hand pointing to EMPTY. Oh boy, that's all she needed. Even now, the motor's making a funny choking noise like it's got something stuck in its windpipe, and what the little lights way down below seem to be telling her is "Goodnight, Sweetheart, Goodnight."

She fumbles in her seat, under it, behind it, finds a pack of cards, a cigar butt, a jar of hair oil, a thumbworn Western, an empty gin bottle (just not her night: even the smell is gone), a plastic ring with a secret code inside, a used bar of soap coated with dustballs, and finally what she's looking for, a parachute. The old crate is wheezing and snorting like a sick mule by now and has already started to take a noser, so she harnesses herself in the chute, flicks the cockpit open, and launches herself out into the starry night, amazed at her own aplomb at such an altitude since even sitting up in the balcony at the movies makes her dizzy.

She's not sure where she's going to land or who's going to be waiting for her or what kind of impression she's going to make, dropping in on them in a cloth cap, moist undies, and a few streamers of bleached-out blouse, but she's hoping the element of surprise will give her the lead time she needs to vanish before they figure out what they've seen. She does wish she had her lost lashes back, though, or at least a tube of lipstick and maybe some deodorant, not to mention the common comb. As though triggered by that thought, the cap flies off and she glances up through her streaming tangle of hair to watch it vanish into the night sky, thinking as she gazes up into the starry dome: wait a minute, something's wrong—*where's the parachute?!* Don't these things open by *themselves?*

Then she remembers something from all those old war movies

about a ring. It's like a window shade or a wedding, you have to put your finger in a ring, then pull. She scrabbles around for it but she can't find it. She can't find *anything* with this dumb thing strapped on her back, she's getting a crick in her neck from trying, so she peels it off and searches it. Nothing. It's like a pillow. Should she just hold it under her and hope for the best? She's dropping so fast! Then she discovers a placket and buttons like a man's fly. She fumbles with the buttons, regretting tearfully, not for the first time in her life, her lack of practice. What she finds inside is a kind of nozzle with a nipple on the end. What? Is she supposed to blow this thing up? This is crazy! She jerks irritably on the nipple, there's a windy hissing sound, and—*pop!*—she finds herself suddenly afloat under a gigantic gas balloon.

Wow! Here she comes, hanging on desperately by one hand and whooshing down over lit-up Main Street, causing cars to screech and crash, dogs to yap hysterically, pedestrians to stumble all over one another in gap-mouthed amazement. She's still too shaken to revel in all this attention, her heart's hammering away in her chest like the drum of a restless native and her nose is either running or bleeding, all she really wants right now is to go sit down somewhere for a few years, even her appetite seems to have failed her. And it's not over yet! She doesn't know how long she can hang on to the nozzle, and the balloon, sweeping down the street toward the movie theater now, seems if anything to be rising again.

Just when all seems lost, her hand sweaty and slipping its grip, the balloon itself caught in a sudden updraft of hot air from the movie lobby which might take her off who knows where, she spies the awning out over the hardware store next door and lets go, dropping onto the awning as though onto a haystack and sliding down it into a pile of rubbish on the curb—not the prettiest of all landings maybe, and a canvas burn or two to remember it by, but she's an all-in-one piece, as her girlfriend would say, she still has her ticket stub, and in the theater the intermission buzzer is just this moment sounding its final warning and everyone is rushing back to his seat.

Luckily the usher is looking the other way as she goes streaking past, the doors swinging closed behind her, the auditorium already dark, some children's cartoon starting up on the screen: loud screeching and banging noises, tinkling music, one animal stomping another one, the usual thing, and distracting enough, she's pretty sure, that no one notices how she's dressed, or rather, not. Her friend has crawled into the row behind and is curled up with the cowboy, her hand in his lap, and just as well because she's too poohed out to put up with any wisecracks just now about all-night suckers or pimple specials or what has she been doing in the ladies' so long, was it fun, can we all do it, who'll bring the buns? Her friend sometimes can be a pain, especially when she's trying to ring some guy's bell.

She scrunches down in her seat, feeling a strange chill and wishing she'd brought along a sweater or something, not to mention some spare bluejeans and an extra pair of shoes. Her teeth start to chatter and her flesh goes all shivery, but it can't be that cold in here, probably it's just nerves (she's never sat this *close* to one of these seats before, so to speak), so she tries to focus on the cartoon to calm herself down. But there's something odd. One of the animals has been twisted into a kind of coiled spring and is boing-boinging around in a way that usually has people hooting and yipping and rolling around in the aisles—but no one's laughing. No one's making *any* kind of sound whatsoever. She twists around uneasily and peeks over the back of her seat: the auditorium, lit only by the light from the projector, is full of people, all right, but they're all sitting stiffly in their seats with weird flattened-out faces, their dilated eyes locked onto the screen like they're hypnotized or dead or something. Uh oh. She reaches back and taps her friend to ask her what she thinks is going on, and her friend, jostled, slides lifelessly off the guy's lap onto the floor between the seats. There's a soft bump, clearly audible under the tinny whistle and crash up on the screen, the burlesque rattle up there as of things tumbling down a thousand stairs. The guy's not looking too great either, just sprawled out there with his cowboy hat down over his nose, his slobbery mouth hanging open,

his belt buckle undone, his hand cupped rigidly around a skinny
behind that isn't there anymore. She's about to let out a yell,
when she feels this icy clawlike grip on her shoulder, and she
can't even squeak. The claw twists her around in her seat until
she's facing the screen again and holds her there, peering up in
the creepy silence at all that hollow tomfoolery and wondering
how she's going to get out of *this* one. If how is the word. It's like
some kind of spell, and there's probably a way to break it, but
right now she can't think of it, she almost can't think at all: it's
like that hoodoo behind her has stuck one of those bony fingers
deep in her ear and pushed the "OFF" button. So what can she
do, she stares up at the screen and pretends to watch the mayhem
(one of the animals, having been pressed into an ice-cube tray, is
now being emptied out in cubes: there are exaggerated pops and
clunks as various bodily parts tumble from the tray), wishing only
that she'd at least picked up that soft drink on the way in, or better yet, a tub of popcorn and a half-dozen chilidogs, it might be a
long night. Like her friend would say, if she were still alive:
"Sometimes, sweetie, you just have to hunker down, spread your
cheeks, and let nature take its curse." Anyway, as far as she can
tell, the claw only wants her to watch the movie, and, hey, she's
been watching movies all her life, so why stop now, right? Besides, isn't there always a happy ending? Has to be. It comes with
the price of the ticket . . .

CARTOON

The cartoon man drives his cartoon car into the cartoon town and runs over a real man. The real man is not badly hurt—the cartoon car is virtually weightless after all, it's hardly any worse than getting a cut lip from licking an envelope—but the real man feels that a wrong has nevertheless been done him, so he goes in search of a policeman. There are no real policemen around, so he takes his complaint to a cartoon policeman. The cartoon policeman salutes him briskly and, almost without turning around, darts off in the direction of the accident, but the real man is disconcerted by the way the policeman hurries along about four inches above the pavement, taking five or six airy steps for every one of his own and blowing his whistle ceaselessly. It's as though they were walking side by side down two different streets. The cartoon town, meanwhile, slides past silently, more or less on its own.

At the scene of the accident, they find the cartoon man with a real policeman. The cartoon car is resting on its roof, looking ill and abused. "Is this the one?" demands the real policeman,

135

pointing with his nightstick. The cartoon man jumps up and down and makes high-pitched incriminating noises, the car snorting and whimpering pathetically in the background. When the cartoon policeman blows his whistle in protest, or perhaps just out of habit, a huge cartoon dog, larger than the cartoon car, bounds onto the scene and chases him off. "You'll have to come with me," announces the real policeman severely, collaring the real man, and he can hear the cartoon car snickering wickedly. "There are procedural matters involved here!"

As though in enactment of this pronouncement, the huge cartoon dog comes lumbering through again from the opposite direction, chased now by a real cat, the cat in turn chased by a cartoon woman. The woman pulls up short upon spying the real policeman, who has meanwhile shot the cat (this is both probable and confounding), and, winking at the real man, bares her breasts for the policeman. These breasts are nearly as large as the woman herself, and they have nipples on them that turn sequentially into pursed lips, dripping spigots, traffic lights, beckoning fingers, then lit-up pinball bumpers. The real policeman is not completely real, after all. He has cartoon eyes that stretch out of their sockets like paired erections, locking on the cartoon woman's breasts with their fanciful nipples. She takes her breasts off and gives them to the real policeman, and he creeps furtively away, clutching the gift closely like a fearful secret, his eyes retracting deep into his skull as though to empty it of its own realness, what's left of it.

"Thank you," says the real man. "You have probably saved my life." He can hear the cartoon car sniggering and wheezing at this, but the cartoon woman simply shrugs and remarks enigmatically: "Plenty more where those came from." She snuggles up to the huge cartoon dog, who has returned and is pawing curiously at the cadaver of the real cat. "I feel somehow," murmurs the dog, sniffing the cat's private parts, "a certain inexplicable anxiety." The cartoon car hoots and wheezes mockingly again, and the dog, annoyed, lifts its leg over it. There is a violent hissing and popping, and then the car is silent. The cartoon man is infuriated at this, squeaking and yipping and beating his fists on the cartoon dog and the cartoon woman. They ignore him, cuddling up once more, the dog panting heavily after exerting himself, both mentally and physically, the woman erotically touching the dog's huge floppy tongue with the tip of her own (she has a real mouth, the real man notices, and the touch of her tiny round tongue against the vast pink landscape of the dog's flat one for some reason makes him want to cry), so the cartoon man scurries over to beat on the real man. It is not so much painful as vaguely unnerving, as though he were being nagged to remember something he had managed to forget.

The cartoon woman drifts off with the cartoon dog ("When," the dog is musing, scratching philosophically behind his ear, "is a flea *not* a flea?"), and the cartoon man, his rage spent, walks over to pick up the dead cat. As the cartoon man walks away, he seems to grow, and when he returns, dragging the dead cat by its tail, he seems to shrink again. He gives the real man a huge cartoon knife, produced as if from nowhere, then dashes off, returning almost instantly with a cartoon table, tablecloth, napkins, plates and silverware, a candelabra, and two cartoon chairs: before these things can even be counted, they are already set in place. His voice makes shrill little speeded-up noises once more, which seem to suggest he wants the real man to cut the cat up for dinner. He zips away again, returning with cartoon salad, steak sauce, and cartoon wine, then streaks off to a cartoon bakery.

Who knows? thinks the real man, tucking in his napkin, all this may be in fulfillment of yet another local ordinance, so more out of respect than appetite, he prepares to cut up the dead cat. When he lays the cat out on the cartoon table, however, all the cartoon plates and silverware, condiments and candelabra leap off the table and run away shrieking, or else laughing, it's hard to tell, and though the table looks horizontal, the cat slides right off it. Oh well, the real man sighs to himself, dropping the knife disconsolately on the table as though paying the check, they can't say I didn't try. He goes over to the cartoon car and sets it on its wheels again and, after a puddle has formed beneath it, gets inside and starts up the motor. Or rather, the motor starts up by it-self, choking and sputtering at first and making loud flatulent noises out its exhaust pipes, then clearing its throat and revving up, eventually humming along smoothly. The cartoon town meanwhile slides by as before.

When they reach the real town, or when the real town, the one where the real man lives, reaches them, the cartoon car doesn't seem to work anymore. The man finds he has to push his feet through the floor and walk it home, much to the apparent amuse-ment of all the real or mostly real passersby. He is reminded of the time when, as a boy, he found himself looking up at his teacher, hovering over him with a humorless smile, wielding a wooden ruler (he thinks of her in retrospect as a cartoon teacher, but he could be mistaken about this—certainly the ruler was real), and accusing him, somewhat mysteriously, of "failing his interpolations." "What?" he'd asked, much to his immediate re-gret, a regret he strangely feels again now, as if he were suffering some kind of spontaneous reenactment, and it suddenly occurs to him, as he walks his cartoon car miserably down the middle of the street through all the roaring real ones, that, yes, the teacher was almost certainly real—but her accusation was a cartoon.

At home he shows his wife, lying listlessly on the sofa, the car-toon car, now no bigger than the palm of his hand, and tells her about his adventures. "It's like being the butt of a joke without a teller or something," he says, casting about for explanations, when, in reality, there probably are none. "I know," she replies with a certain weary bitterness. She lifts her skirts and shows him the cartoon man. "He's been there all day." The cartoon man smirks up at him over his shoulder, making exaggerated under-cranked thrusts with his tiny cartoon buttocks, powder white with red spots like a clown's cheeks. "Is he . . . he hurting you?" the real man gasps. "No, it just makes me jittery. It's sort of like cut-ting your lip on the edge of an envelope," she adds with a grim-ace, letting her skirt drop, "if you know what I mean."

"Ah . . ." He too feels a stinging somewhere, though perhaps only in his reflections. Distantly, he hears a policeman's whistle, momentarily persuasive, but he knows this is no solution, real or otherwise. It would be like scratching an itch with legislation or an analogy—something that cartoon dog might have said and perhaps did, he wasn't listening all the time. No, one tries, but it's never enough. With a heavy heart (what a universe!), he goes into the bathroom to flush the cartoon car down the toilet and discovers, glancing in the mirror, that, above the cartoon napkin still tucked into his collar like a lolling tongue, he seems to have grown a pair of cartoon ears. They stick out from the sides of his head like butterfly wings. Well, well, he thinks, wagging his new ears animatedly, or perhaps being wagged by them, there's hope for me yet . . .

MILFORD JUNCTION, 1939:
A Brief Encounter

It comes, in the damp night, as if out of nowhere, roaring up out of the raw empty silence with a sudden shriek, as though of pain, or rapture, or perhaps mere surprise, amazed at being here, here in the Milford Junction railway station (such an ordinary place, the most ordinary place in the world, really, and yet . . .), or, rather, amazed to be passing through it, for it doesn't stop, the boat train never stops, that's just the trouble with it, as the people down on Milford High Street will often remark, it can be quite dangerous, careening through here with its sudden violent scream, its thunderous *rum! rum! rum!* like the sounding of heavy chords, whipping up dust and newsprint and old ticket stubs, expelling vast clouds of steam and smoke, forcing passengers for other trains away from the edge of the platform, casting flickering lights from the windows on them as though slapping their wan faces with the intermittent tick of time itself, reminding them of their insignificance (the train is not stopping, not for them), and throwing out bits of grit and cinder from its billowing smoke that can lodge in a person's eye if he or she is not careful, a nasty business, a very nasty business.

And then, as quickly as it has arrived—a moment no longer than a greeting, really, a furtive kiss, the pouring of a cup of tea—it is gone, rumbling away into the infinite darkness whence it came, leaving in its wake a strange hollow silence in which can be heard the soft fall of resettling litter, a gasp, or perhaps a sigh, steps hurrying through the underpasses. The pale swirling clouds of steam and smoke left behind obscure everything, as though insisting, at least for the moment, upon a complete erasure of all that has preceded the boat train's hurtling passage, but soon enough they dissolve and the old familiar structures reemerge, as of course (though not without their own aura of mystery) they must: the posts and girders, gates, electric lamps, hanging clock, the signs (REFRESHMENT ROOM, WAY OUT, CAPSTAN CIGARETTES, MILFORD JUNCTION), the directional signals and warning lights, anonymous sheds and towers, and here, facing each other across the gleaming rails between them like mirrored stages, the pairs of canopied platforms with their benches and railings, heavy wooden carts of stacked luggage, vending machines and hoardings, their pools of dull light and deep shadows, their incessant drama of arrival and departure.

There is more to this lively market town, to be sure, than its railway station. Indeed, the citizens of Milford do not really think of the station at Milford Junction as part of their town at all, but rather as a sort of outer gate through which flow all the people who come here from the villages around, drawn to the bustling High Street with its chemists, gift shops, cafés, cinemas, and tobacconists—on sunny days, there's even the occasional barrel organist, playing such old favorites as "Let the Great Big World Keep Turning"—to do their week's shopping, change their library books, have lunch together, perhaps go to the pictures. There are factories here and coal mines, a widely admired war memorial, even a famous hospital for the treatment of the specific form of pneumoconiosis known as anthracosis. It's all perfectly ordinary perhaps to those who live here, but quite thrilling, you know, if you're from some place like Churley or Ketchworth. Milford: it's like a magical storybook place, just waiting to be filled up, to be, for one wildly happy moment (though it can't last of course, nothing lasts, really) *inhabited*—just the name alone makes you feel like laughing! It's like watching the pictures and being *in* them at the same time, as though one might be able somehow to eat the world with one's eyes, if that's not too idiotic. Milford! Well, it's easy to be a little foolish in a place like this. There are wonderful botanical gardens with lakes on which swans preen and small boys sail their boats, and picturesque pathways where nannies push their prams, and landing stages for rowboats and canals with funny low bridges and lovely old boathouses along the shore. With luck, after a brisk row, one can get a cup of tea from the boatman, warm up around his potbellied Ideal boiler, dry out wet clothing, if there is any, have a little chat. And just beyond Milford, there's the countryside with its stone bridges and pretty little streams and pubs and wintry hills—pleasures that are at once innocent and yet quite terrifying, as though this gentle landscape might contain dreadful precipices, dangerously alluring abysses into which one might, in a moment of utter but delicious madness, throw oneself. Well, in a manner of speaking, of course.

But at night all this vanishes and there is only the Milford Junction railway station. It's almost as though the citizens of Milford might be mistaken: as though the market town of which they're so proud might be little more than a theatrical performance put on each day for the customers giving up their tickets on arrival at the Milford Junction Station barrier, then folding up each night as the customers return, a setting as ephemeral, as phantasmal as those of the afternoon pictures down at the Palladium or the Palace. One approaches the station by way of an overpass with a rather splendid view through the tall iron fence (if one is not too preoccupied to notice) of the lights of the town, seen through the steam billowing up from the railway tracks below like fog on the moors, casting huge cloudy symbols, as it were (one thinks, if one's a poetry addict, unavoidably of Keats), and other strange illusions into the air, along with those bits of grit which sometimes get in people's eyes. A long descent follows, as though to suggest a sinking of the heart, even though it's been a lovely day and one's just had such fun—of course, that's part of the difficulty, isn't it, one so looks forward to these days in Milford, and then, hardly before they've begun, they're already over, it doesn't seem to be any time at all: yet another reminder (as if one needed reminding!) that nothing, not even life, lasts very long. It's enough to bring tears to one's eyes, and sometimes does, never mind the grit and the rest of it.

The platforms are reached by way of the large booking hall and the ticket barrier, manned as always by Mr. Godby, and then, if one's destination so requires, by a further descent through subterranean underpasses, noted for their harsh triangulated lighting, the litter blowing through them whenever the trains rumble overhead, the couples kissing furtively in shadowy niches even as they hurry through, as though the faintly shameful atmosphere of these bowel-like passages had, however briefly, to be tasted. On the platforms themselves, silhouetted figures can be seen, dressed in ordinary macs or belted trenchcoats, leaning on posts, reading newspapers, perhaps sitting on benches, smoking pipes and cigarettes. Others walk in and out of the puddles of light cast by the dull bulbs above, umbrellas and overnight cases in their hands or purses under their arms, checking their watches, showing signs of impatience and fatigue, appearing and disappearing like actors moving on and off stage, an inexpressibly vulgar observation perhaps, yet somehow as irresistible in this peculiarly detached place as those stolen kisses in the subways below. When trains come and go, there is a sudden surge of acitivity as people clatter hastily through the underpasses, jump on and off trains, exchange frantic hugs and kisses and farewell glances, and then there are whistles and loud hissings, the slamming of carriage doors, shouts, the rolling of steel wheels, the extraction of last-minute promises ("Next Thursday!" "Yes, next Thursday!"), and the trains rumble out of the station, their taillights vanishing into the dark. In the ensuing silence, the remaining passengers lean once more against posts, or pace back and forth through the pools of light, while porters push carts of luggage past, and stationmasters check their watches, then cross the tracks on foot, hop up on platform number 2 and 3, and, following the pointing hand sil-

houetted on the sign above, enter the refreshment room for a cup
of tea.

Eventually, of course, one will arrive home in Ketchworth or
Churley, or wherever, to husbands and wives, a sick child perhaps, children certainly, well or ill, problems with maids, the un-
wrapping of packages and stories about Milford ("I meant to do
it, Fred, I really meant to do it!" "Good for you!"), a bit of pro-
vincial social life or else a quiet supper at home, then the latest
book from Boots perhaps, some music on the wireless, crossword
puzzles or house calls (if one's a general practitioner, for example), the obligatory sewing basket from which wild horses can't
seem to drag one, and finally off to bed—but, first, before board-
ing the homebound train, there's almost always time for a cup of
tea in the refreshment room at Milford Junction Station. Indeed,
a day in Milford is not quite complete without it—an overly long
film at the Palladium or an encounter with gossiping acquaintances who talk and talk and talk till one wants to strangle them,
then a flying last-minute dash to the station just as the train is
pulling in and no time for tea, why, it simply spoils everything.

Not that there's anything special about the refreshment room;
it's quite common, really, with pale walls, dark woodwork, arched
doors and windows, the glazing opaqued with REFRESHMENT ROOM
stamped out in reverse, plain wooden tables and bentwood chairs
scattered about, an old iron coal stove in the middle of the room,
and a small bar and tea counter to one side, the sort of room
where the tea is served with too much milk in it, the sandwiches
and buns, in spite of all the claims to the contrary, are usually
stale, where there's a constant draft, no place even to powder
your nose, and the staff is addicted to Three Star brandy. Yet it is
possible to be quite ordinarily contented in here, to be at peace,
which is no small thing and perhaps all one can really hope for if
one wants to be able to go home again and all for the price of a
mere cup of tea. Of course, one can well imagine a room such as
this, perched out here on a railway platform, a kind of island upon
an island, as a likely place for chance encounters, new friend-
ships, even high romance, together with all the desperate happi-

ness and misery that might be expected to follow upon reckless-
ness of that sort, but for the most part the people who come and
go here are sensible persons, even rather withdrawn and shy and
difficult (the climate is said to have something to do with this),
and they have little interest in meeting strangers or even in running into old acquaintances. They are too tired. They are here to
rest, to refresh themselves before the long trip home, that's why
it's called a refreshment room. They purchase their cup of tea and
perhaps a Bath bun or some chocolate, and toddle wearily to an
empty table, there to hover privately over their steaming cup and
smoke a cigarette, perhaps read a book or a newspaper, poke
through their purse, do their face a bit, glancing up only to ob-
serve, idly, as though daydreaming, the exits and entrances of
others, or to watch the woman at the counter going on as usual,
the one with the refined voice. Now and then, mind you, there are
irresponsible people who don't behave themselves, people who
suddenly start showing high spirits and acting quite dotty, coming
back into the refreshment room, having missed their trains, pretending they've forgotten something, behaving rather too vehe-
mently like romantic schoolgirls or excited schoolboys, grasping
at each other, crying out, utterly dazed and bewildered, com-
plaining of grit in their eyes, or whatever, becoming a trifle ill actually, even occasionally doing violence to themselves, to their
hearts and minds and the rest as well, throwing themselves under
the speeding boat train, or more likely right under the tables, en-
gaging in rather undignified scuffling, as one might call it, too
overwhelmed by their feelings even to remove their macs and
fur-lined topcoats, their wet socks and shoes and dreadfully hu-
miliating garter belts ("There's still time!" one of them may be
gasping, as though in pain, or rapture, or perhaps mere surprise,
the other replying: "We're only middle-aged once, there's no
time at all!"), their hats falling over their eyes as the tables and
teacups tumble down around their ears ("Beryl," the woman at
the counter is accustomed to call out over these annoying distur-
bances, her handkerchief to her nose, just as the stovepipe perhaps comes crashing down, as it is all too inclined to do, coal dust

billowing about everywhere, spoiling the buns and tea, and capa-
ble, as is well known, of getting in one's lungs and causing anthracosis, "ask Mr. Godby to come here for a moment, would you?"),
all in all a most appalling exhibition of mad violent energy and
blind frustration and a deep-rooted, unsentimental, but very
naughty desire to reveal hidden depths, and as soon as possible—"Oh, look out! We can't get through!" "Pull on your left!"
"Oh dear, I never could tell left from—!" "Darling!" "No!
Please, not quite yet!" "I must!" And then, almost immediately,
time and tide waiting for no man, as the counter lady would say
with characteristic disdain, looking down her nose at the both of
them, their otherwise quite insignificant lives suddenly experience the most agonizing inflation together with frightful cross-
eyed spasms that send the coal scuttle flying and creating an
awful uproar, and then, as quickly as it has begun, it is over (it's
hardly credible that it should be so short a time!), they are falling
apart and into a kind of trance, as one might describe it (is the
room tilting?), having a sort of idiotic fainting spell, and unable to
think of anything at all to say in the strange hollow silence afterwards, except maybe, "It's been so very nice, I've enjoyed my afternoon enormously," or "How kind it was of you to take so much
trouble." "Nothing at all. There's my train, I must go—good-
bye."

   Well, by the time Mr. Godby has come in, of course, with his
cheery "Hullo, hullo, hullo! What's goin' on in here?", his lips
pursed and his thumbs thrust solemnly in his vest pockets, the
5:40 to Churley is already pulling out of the number 4 platform
across the way and the Ketchworth train, due to depart at 5:43, is
arriving on platform number 3—the great world keeps turning,
after all, and no harm done ("Come along now, what are you
standin' there gapin' at? And Beryl, put some more coals on the
stove while you're at it!"), even the boat train, careening through,
has claimed no new victims, it's been just another ordinary evening in the Milford Junction railway station. Out on the platform,
carriage doors are slamming, windows are being lowered for last-
minute farewells ("Next Thursday, the same time?"), whistles are

blowing and the loudspeakers are announcing imminent depar-
tures and arrivals. Passengers inside the train compartments are
lifting their packages and luggage onto overhead racks or planting them on empty seats, hoping the train is not going to be too
packed, getting out books and newspapers for the dreary ride
home (yes, one *does* have one's roots), exchanging greetings with
acquaintances, if there are any, or perhaps with perfect strangers,
more as a matter of politeness, really, than for any other reason,
then settling back for a last glance out at the Milford Junction
Station (Mr. Godby can be seen in the refreshment room, where
there seems to have been a bit of a dustup, though now he's
merely sipping tea, perhaps conversing with the woman behind
the counter or slapping her bum, as he's inclined to do whenever
he's in high spirits or else miserably in love, overwhelmed by the
flames of passion and other dangerous feelings, which in the end,
if you're not used to them, are rather too much like being sick on
a channel steamer, frankly, even if they do make something of a
change), the platforms already beginning to slide away into the
night like the last of the rolling titles in a picture show at the Palladium, the shadowy figures on the platforms now little more than
some nameless creatures who have no reality at all and who soon
vanish altogether, the accelerating landscape, framed by the train
window, gradually receding into a kind of distant panoramic
backdrop for one's own dreams and memories, projected onto the
strange blurry space in between, which is more or less where the
window is, but is not the window itself, a rather peculiar space
perhaps, somehow there and not there at the same time, but no
less real, my dear, for all that and, at the very least, a fascinating
place in which to lose oneself for just a little while, just a little
while, on the way home to Churley or Ketchworth, until someone,
meaning to be kind, gives you a shake and says, quite soberly and
cruelly, "Wake up! We're here!" and (it's almost happening already) all those silly dreams disappear . . .

TOP HAT

Uniformed men move in a dark choral mass at the foot of an iron tower under unlit lamps, their top hats squared, their shadowed faces anonymous and interchangeable. They suggest power without themselves possessing it, moving with ceremonial precision, otherwise silent, their secret motives concealed. They seem to want their walking sticks, carried like emblems of the elect, to speak for them.

Suddenly their decorum is shattered, as out of the vanishing point of the night a new figure emerges, strolling jauntily into their midst as though a door were being opened, light thrown, a die cast: they all fall back. At first glance, he might seem to be one of their own: he too wears top hat and tails, white tie, spats, carries a stick. But he is dressed like them and not like them: the top hat is tilted defiantly over one ear, the walking stick twirls like a vulgar unriddling of sacrament, his lapels are pulled back to show more of his snowy white breast by a hand flicking in and out of his pants pocket like a lizard's tongue. He is unmistakably (his face is lit up with an open disarming grin, he is a loner and extravagant and his grip is firm) an outsider here. And he means to offend.

The others close ranks behind him as though to seal a wound, watch him apprehensively. Perhaps he *is* one of them, as yet unformed. Is this possible? As though in reply, that frisky hand takes another dip, emerges this time with a scrap of paper: "I've just got an invitation through the mail," he crows, wagging the paper about like a press release. They lean on their sticks, studying this strutting intruder: perhaps they find heresy momentarily fascinating. Perhaps this is a weakness. "Your presence requested this evening, it's formal, top hat, white tie, and tails!" He has been slapping the paper with his walking stick as though it were a sales pitch, a sermon, a writ, but now he wads it up and impiously—the men behind him stiffen, their walking sticks gripped tightly between their legs—tosses it away. Credentials? Hey, who needs them? He twirls his stick and swaggers up and down in front of them, grinningly mocking their vestments, their rituals, their very raison d'être, as the natives might say. "And I trust you'll excuse my dust when I step on the gas!" he laughs, beating back their tentative lockstep challenge with a cocky, limbs-akimbo reply of his own.

There is an indignant bang of walking sticks, bringing him to a halt. He hesitates, then shrugs as though to say, oh well, when in Rome (if that's where he is), even if they're crazy—and (maybe, deep down, this is what he truly wants, it's not much fun being a loner in this world, after all, even if you are number one) joins the others in a formal strut. But not for long. He just doesn't fit in somehow. They turn away, perhaps to lead him back where he came from, but he's in no mood to go home yet. Not like this. He follows them for a step or two, but then, as though overcoming temptation (all social forms are conspiracies in the end, are they not?), breaks away and, shoulders bobbing and hips swiveling, lets them know who he really is. He drums it out loud and clear with stick, heels, and toes, all four limbs rapping away at once, then plants the walking stick as though claiming turf. They watch impassively, their own sticks discreetly concealed. He restates his dissent, even more emphatically, elbows out and pumping as though he might be trying to take off.

He pauses. Has he won his case? He looks back over his shoulder. No, they are not even impressed. They repeat his sequence, but staidly and en masse. It's a kind of reprimand: the movement is possible, technically anyway, but unbridled egoism is not. He insists, throwing himself into ever more unorthodox convulsions, his walking stick flicking around his head like a cracked whip. He is incorrigible. A barbarian, a peacock. He does not even seem completely white. They leave him.

Or maybe I somehow wished them away, reversed them out of my life like a rejected fairytale, a shabby dream, just as, for all I knew, I might well have wished them here in the first place. I was far from home; anything seemed possible. Certainly they vanished like shadows, leaving these strange streets bathed in a fresh light that lifted my spirits. I knew time was passing because I could hear my hands and feet tick-tocking away below, but the sensation I had was of a languorous serenity, a delicious pause between clocked anxieties. My life was changing, but for a moment it was standing still.

I may have got carried away a bit by the sheer enchantment of it, for, alone now, I could feel my body shed its weight suddenly and burst into an almost uncontrollable spasm of hip-twisting exuberance. Perhaps I meant it as an affront: their tails hung down, mine had to fly! Even as I dutifully planted my walking stick, my feet—I seemed to have at least four of them, all rattling at once—kicked it away. The stick took on a life of its own, whirling me giddily round and round as it whipped at the hard ground, sliced the air. I'd never known anything quite like it. I felt like I was about to blow my doggone hat off.

I knew that I had come to this place to change my life. Or that, somehow, because my life had to change, I had come to this place. The invitation seemed to suggest this: it was a special occasion. But, even as I found myself suddenly spinning dizzily around my rooted walking stick, I could not imagine what the nature of that change could be. Perhaps it had to do with the old men (I seemed to remember old men), or perhaps with the place itself, a place that seemed to be there and not to be there at the same time, like an unwritten melody, more an aura than a place, barren and seductive and overhung with melancholic storm clouds. And growing ominously dark . . .

Wait! I stopped, staggered drunkenly, spread my legs to keep from falling. What place *was* this? What exactly was I *doing* here? I tucked my elbows in. I'd taken that invitation for granted: but who had sent it? I couldn't remember. Perhaps I'd never known. I looked up at the louring sky, gripping my walking stick with both hands, feeling bereft, forgotten. Yet liking the feel of the stick. The streetlamps had come on. And under them, a girl stood. "I suppose," she said, staring at my feet, which were, though I had little to do with it, still on the move, "it's some kind of affliction."

"Yes, yes," I stammered, "it's—it's an affliction . . ." I lowered my walking stick. Her caustic twang, so far from home, had startled me. She had genuine melting-pot lard in her cheeks and hips, her negligee was swank, but it was also vulgar, straight off Main Street, and she had the crusty don't-number-two-me worldliness of the girl-next-door. I felt I had seen her somewhere before. I began to perceive the nature of my trial.

I was in a foreign place. The light was bad but I could see plain enough this guy was not one of the locals. The fancy duds were right but they fit him funny, like he was growing into them and out of them at the same time. He was playing with that swagger stick of his like he was trying to jerk it off, and I had the impression from the way he gaped at me that about all he could register for the moment was two tits and a tongue. Right away he starts mooning about his nursies, by which I supposed he meant his old lady, this john being strictly backwater, soup and fish notwith-

standing—I mean, he had some pretty fancy moves, but all that
nimble-footedness looked to me like something he mighta learned
tippytoeing through the cowshit. It was my guess that the nearest
he'd had to a nursemaid was some old Gran out on the prairie
who'd spooned him baked squash, rhubarb pie, and get-up-and-go
marketplace fairytales, but bull's wool or no, the message was
clear: this guy wanted his mommy.

The weird thing was how he couldn't stop jiggering about. It
was like somebody had wound him up, then thrown away the key.
Was it those old guys up in the balcony? I'd come on him spinning
round and round his planted stick like he was in love with it. His
dick, sure, I thought, but more than that: it was like some hole in
the middle that he could circle round all day but never get inside
of, and it was driving him crazy. "I'm free, that's me," he was
hollering, and it was scaring him spitless. When he finally tucked
his stick back in his clothes, he was staggering so he could hardly
stand up—yet his feet kept ticky-tocking away under him like he
had the St. Vitus dance or something. So I spoke up. I said I supposed it was some kind of affliction, and he said it was and in fact
he really shouldn't be left alone. I could see that, and suggested a
couple of guards. I had to admit there was something attractive
about him, though, in spite of his being a wanker and a loony.
Maybe I was just homesick. Or tired of trying to get by in these
hard times as a rich dressmaker's whore: there's a side to this
kind of glamour that most people don't see. And it ain't the front
side. Whatever the reason, when he launched into a little birds-
and-bees number about "a clumsy cloud and a fluffy little cloud"
(was he kidding? maybe all he'd had to shag till now were sheep
. . .), I found myself thinking, oh well, what the hell, though I
don't know the yokel from Adam, I just might let him scud up to a
pap if it'd make him feel any better. If only he'd stop weewawing
around like that.

And that was when these guys showed up.

Don't ask me who they were. I'm not even sure *what* they
were. They came rising up out of the ground like from you-know-
where. And you could tell these greasers meant business. Fluffy
little clouds, my fanny, I thought, that boy shoulda stayed home

on the farm! He looked like he was about to poop marbles, hunkered down there with his willow between his legs and his hat squashing his big ears out. Even his twitchy feet had gone dead on him. I figured the rube was done for and was just starting to feel sorry for him, when whaddaya know! he suddenly rears up, turns that little white-tipped stick of his into some kind of magical popgun, and starts mowing down the lot of them! Rappy-tappy-tap, down they go, blood and brains blowing everywhere, it's a fantastic rub-out! Hey, I thought, this guy is *good!*

They return as they left: as though compelled. Arising like plants from the soil. Have they been called back because of the girl? To present her perhaps with a moral alternative? Or to recall *him* to the world of men? They bring with them, certainly, the aura of purpose, of culture, law, of subjection of the will to the greater beauty of the whole, but this aura rests upon them more like an affliction than a promise. Or perhaps it's just those preposterous squared-off hats.

They pause, standing in a row like soldiers at ease, their walking sticks planted between their legs, their white-gloved hands clasped at the heads as though protecting their genitals. Or pointing to them. They seem ready to serve, yet uncertain as to the nature of their service. Is he to join their ranks? Is she to embellish them? Or are they mere witnesses to a drama from which they are—ontologically, as it were—excluded? He provides an answer of sorts: he raises his walking stick and, pointing it like a fairground rifle, shoots one of their number: p-*tang!* The man crumples and falls, clutching at the sky.

Nothing changes. And everything changes. The outsider, it seems, is here to kill. And they, his hosts, are here to die. Possessed suddenly of an amazing and exemplary grace, he executes them one by one, but after the first surprise, there is no other: p-*tang!* p-*tang!*—down they go, grabbing at their breasts, their faces, reaching desperately for the darkening sky.

The girl meanwhile is falling madly in love—or perhaps is at last being rejoined with her true love—her face lit up now with a kind of mystical ecstasy. She falls into step with him, moving in adoring concert, yet never touching, discovering—or rediscovering—an essential affinity, a zest for life and art—p-*tang!* p-*tang!*—innately shared. He fires from over his head, drops them two at a time from the hip, even lifts his leg and shoots from under it, as though to deepen the humiliation of their ineluctable and spellbound deaths. She moves among the victims, her heels rapping out a pitter-patter of termination, flouncing her skirts like the dropping of final curtains.

He knocks another one down, shooting blindly over his shoulder, then, holding the stick at his belly—*ruckety-tackety-tuckety-tack!*—impatiently machine-guns the lot. The dying men whirl and writhe, blood jetting from their bodies like the release of some inner effervescence. Their executioner, grown tall, staggers momentarily as though drunk with pleasure, turns wide-eyed toward the girl. She draws near to complete their final figure, which would seem, by the expression on her face, to be nothing short of orgasm (perhaps it is already overtaking her, as his arms reach out she is rolling to her back, her eyes closed, mouth agape)—

But wait! there's one still standing! This one seems smaller somehow, or else more remote, planted at the foot of the iron tower like a flaw in the visitor's own character, hands clasped soberly at the head of his stick. The visitor drops the girl (she gasps, grabbing herself as she falls), draws himself erect, and, his boyish grin frozen on his face, fires: the man leans to one side, ducking the shot, and says: "I know what you're trying to do, my friend, and I don't want to take the wind out of your sails, but perhaps, in your pursuit of untrammeled happiness, you have been a little imprudent. For there *are* dates that cannot be broken, and words, you know, that cannot be spoken. This is more than a clash of taste, a bit of a tiff. You are seeking, through murder—"

His executioner, sweating now though still grinning widely, teeth clamped in what is either manly determination or unbridled terror (the girl, groaning, convulses ambivalently at his feet), fires again: the man calmly leans the other way and continues,

"You are seeking, as I say, through murder, to overcome that ambivalence at the heart of your quest, but what you are killing is merely something in yourself. Indeed, it is unlikely that, when the killing is done, there can possibly be anything left. You cannot celebrate, my friend, what does not exist. There is no Adam, for all your wishful thinking, and there never was; those treacherous brothers just made that up to account for their discontent. Yours is a grave misapprehension, with consequences far beyond your hasty actions here. Believe me, a few technical skills, gutsiness, and a silly smile will not resolve——"

Enraged, the newcomer bounces his swagger stick off the street and, as though to argue the case for personal ingenuity and pluck (it's *not* just technology, blast it, it's a whole new *spirit*——!), grabs it on the rebound and raises it like an Indian's bow. "Wait!" cries the man at the foot of the tower. The overhanging globes are so aligned as to seem to be pointing to his chest. "Hear me out!" The girl can be seen crawling away into the shadows in her glossy negligee, perhaps to sleep awhile, and dream. "I admit your instincts are sound, but your methods are ingenuous! It's not *whose* hats, but who's——!" His opponent draws the bow——or seems to: there is a mystery about the arrow——and lets it go. There is a crack like a rifle shot, the man at the tower cries out: *"No, no, damn it! SHOOT THE OLD ME-E-E-e-ennn——!"* and, flinging an arm in the air, crumples, his face falling into shadows.

The intruder is alone now on the street, except for all the bodies, those bitten apples, heaped about like cairns, like gates for a dance routine. The night has deepened. He tucks the stick under his arm, straightens his white tie, brushes off his tails, as though recollecting an old code. He looks at his feet: they are quiet at last. He grins at this, and shrugs, waggles his hips. In the heavy silence (he will never, never change), he doffs his hat and takes his spidery bow.

YOU MUST REMEMBER THIS

I t is dark in Rick's apartment. Black leader dark, heavy and abstract, silent but for a faint hoarse crackle like a voiceless plaint, and brief as sleep. Then Rick opens the door and the light from the hall scissors in like a bellboy to open up space, deposit surfaces (there is a figure in the room), harbinger event (it is Ilsa). Rick follows, too preoccupied to notice: his café is closed, people have been shot, he has troubles. But then, with a stroke, he lights a small lamp (such a glow! the shadows retreat, *every-thing* retreats: where are the walls?) and there she is, facing him, holding open the drapery at the far window like the front of a nightgown, the light flickering upon her white but determined face like static. Rick pauses for a moment in astonishment. Ilsa lets the drapery and its implications drop, takes a step forward into the strangely fretted light, her eyes searching his.

"How did you get in?" he asks, though this is probably not the question on his mind.

"The stairs from the street."

This answer seems to please him. He knows how vulnerable he

is, after all, it's the way he lives—his doors are open, his head is bare, his tuxedo jacket is snowy white—that's not important. What matters is that by such a reply a kind of destiny is being fulfilled. Sam has a song about it. "I told you this morning you'd come around," he says, curling his lips as if to advertise his appetite for punishment, "but this is a little ahead of schedule." She faces him squarely, broad-shouldered and narrow-hipped, a sash around her waist like a gun belt, something shiny in her tensed left hand. He raises both his own as if to show they are empty: "Well, won't you sit down?"

His offer, whether in mockery or no, releases her. Her shoulders dip in relief, her breasts; she sweeps forward (it is only a small purse she is carrying: a toothbrush perhaps, cosmetics, her hotel key), her face softening: "Richard!" He starts back in alarm, hands moving to his hips. "I had to see you!"

"So you use Richard again!" His snarling retreat throws up a barrier between them. She stops. He pushes his hands into his pockets as though to reach for the right riposte: "We're back in Paris!"

That probably wasn't it. Their song seems to be leaking into the room from somewhere out in the night, or perhaps it has been there all the time—Sam maybe, down in the darkened bar, sending out soft percussive warnings in the manner of his African race: "Think twice, boss. Hearts fulla passion, you c'n rely. Jealousy, boss, an' hate. Le's go fishin'. Sam."

"Please!" she begs, staring at him intently, but he remains unmoved:

"Your unexpected visit isn't connected by any chance with the letters of transit?" He ducks his head, his upper lip swelling with bitterness and hurt. "It seems as long as I have those letters, I'll never be lonely."

Yet, needless to say, he will always be lonely—in fact, this is the confession ("You can ask any price you want," she is saying) only half-concealed in his muttered subjoinder: Rick Blaine is a loner, born and bred. Pity him. There is this lingering, almost primal image of him, sitting alone at a chessboard in his white tuxedo, smoking contemplatively in the midst of a raucous conniving crowd, a crowd he has himself assembled about him. He taps a pawn, moves a white knight, fondles a tall black queen while a sardonic smile plays on his lips. He seems to be toying, self-mockingly, with Fate itself, as indifferent toward Rick Blaine (never mind that he says—as he does now, turning away from her— that *"I'm* the only cause *I'm* interested in . . .") as toward the rest of the world. It's all shit, so who cares?

Ilsa is staring off into space, a space that a moment ago Rick filled. She seems to be thinking something out. The negotiations are going badly; perhaps it is this she is worried about. He has just refused her offer of "any price," ignored her ultimatum ("You *must* giff me those letters!"), sneered at her husband's heroism, and scoffed at the very cause that first brought them together in Paris. How could he do that? And now he has abruptly turned his back on her (does he think it was just sex? what has happened to him since then?) and walked away toward the balcony door, meaning, apparently, to turn her out. She takes a deep breath, presses her lips together, and, clutching her tiny purse with both hands, wheels about to pursue him: "Richard!" This has worked before, it works again: he turns to face her new approach: "We luffed each other once . . ." Her voice catches in her throat, tears come to her eyes. She is beautiful there in the slatted shadows, her hair loosening around her ears, eyes glittering, throat bare and vulnerable in the open V-neck of her ruffled blouse. She's a good dresser. Even that little purse she squeezes: so like the other one, so lovely, hidden away. She shakes her head slightly in wistful appeal: "If those days meant . . . anything at all to you . . ."

"I wouldn't bring up Paris if I were you," he says stonily. "It's poor salesmanship."

She gasps (*she* didn't bring it up: is he a madman?), tosses her head back: "Please! Please listen to me!" She closes her eyes, her lower lip pushed forward as though bruised. "If you knew what really happened, if you only knew the truth—!"

He stands over this display, impassive as a Moorish executioner (that's it! he's turning into one of these bloody Arabs, she thinks). "I wouldn't believe you, no matter what you told me," he says. In Ethiopia, after an attempt on the life of an Italian officer, he saw 1600 Ethiopians get rounded up one night and shot in reprisal. Many were friends of his. Or clients anyway. But somehow her deceit is worse. "You'd say anything now, to get what you want." Again he turns his back on her, strides away.

She stares at him in shocked silence, as though all that had happened eighteen months ago in Paris were flashing suddenly before her eyes, now made ugly by some terrible revelation. An exaggerated gasp escapes her like the breaking of wind: his head snaps up and he turns sharply to the right. She chases him, dogging his heels. "You want to feel sorry for yourself, don't you?" she cries and, surprised (he was just reaching for something on an ornamental table, the humidor perhaps), he turns back to her. "With so much at stake, all you can think off is your own feeling," she rails. Her lips are drawn back, her breathing labored, her eyes watering in anger and frustration. "One woman has hurt you, and you take your reffenge on the rest off the world!" She is choking, she can hardly speak. Her accent seems to have got worse. "You're a coward, und veakling, und—"

She gasps. What is she saying? He watches her, as though faintly amused. "No, Richard, I'm sorry!" Tears are flowing in earnest now: she's gone too far! This is the expression on her face. She's in a corner, struggling to get out. "I'm sorry, but—" She wipes the tears from her cheek, and calls once again on her husband, that great and courageous man whom they both admire, whom the whole world admires: "—you're our last hope! If you don't help us, Victor Laszlo will die in Casablanca!"

"What of it?" he says. He has been waiting for this opportunity. He plays with it now, stretching it out. He turns, reaches for a cigarette, his head haloed in the light from an arched doorway. "I'm gonna die in Casablanca. It's a good spot for it." This line is meant to be amusing, but Ilsa reacts with horror. Her eyes widen. She catches her breath, turns away. He lights up, pleased with himself, takes a practiced drag, blows smoke. "Now," he says, turning toward her, "if you'll—"

He pulls up short, squints: she has drawn a revolver on him. So much for toothbrushes and hotel keys. "All right. I tried to reason with you. I tried effrything. Now I want those letters." Distantly, a melodic line suggests a fight for love and glory, an ironic case of do or die. "Get them for me."

"I don't have to." He touches his jacket. "I got 'em right here."

"Put them on the table."

He smiles and shakes his head. "No." Smoke curls up from the cigarette he is holding at his side like the steam that enveloped the five o'clock train to Marseilles. Her eyes fill with tears. Even as she presses on ("For the last time . . . !"), she knows that "no" is final. There is, behind his ironic smile, a profound sadness, the fatalistic survivor's wistful acknowledgment that, in the end, the fundamental things apply. Time, going by, leaves nothing behind, not even moments like this. "If Laszlo and the cause mean so much," he says, taunting her with her own uncertainties, "you won't stop at anything . . ."

He seems almost to recede. The cigarette disappears, the smoke. His sorrow gives way to something not unlike eagerness. "All right, I'll make it easier for you," he says, and walks toward her. "Go ahead and shoot. You'll be doing me a favor."

She seems taken aback, her eyes damp, her lips swollen and parted. Light licks at her face. He gazes steadily at her from his superior moral position, smoke drifting up from his hand once more, his white tuxedo pressed against the revolver barrel. Her eyes close as the gun lowers, and she gasps his name: "Richard!" It is like an invocation. Or a profession of faith. "I tried to stay away," she sighs. She opens her eyes, peers up at him in abject surrender. A tear moves slowly down her cheek toward the corner of her mouth like secret writing. "I thought I would neffer see you again . . . that you were out off my life . . ." She blinks, cries out faintly—"Oh!"—and (he seems moved at last, his mask of disdain falling away like perspiration) turns away, her head wrenched to one side as though in pain.

Stricken with sudden concern, or what looks like concern, he steps up behind her, clasping her breasts with both hands, nuzzling in her hair. "The day you left Paris. . . !" she sobs, though she seems unsure of herself. One of his hands is already down between her legs, the other inside her blouse, pulling a breast out of its brassiere cup. "If you only knew . . . what I . . ." He is moaning, licking at one ear, the hand between her legs nearly lifting her off the floor, his pelvis bumping at her buttocks. "Is this . . . right?" she gasps.

"I—I don't know!" he groans, massaging her breast, the nipple between two fingers. "I can't think!"

"But . . . you *must* think!" she cries, squirming her hips. Tears are streaming down her cheeks now. "For . . . for . . ."

"What?" he gasps, tearing her blouse open, pulling on her breast as though to drag it over her shoulder where he might kiss it. Or eat it: he seems ravenous suddenly.

"I . . . I can't remember!" she sobs. She reaches behind to jerk at his fly (what else is she to do, for the love of Jesus?), then rips away her sash, unfastens her skirt, her fingers trembling.

"Holy shit!" he wheezes, pushing his hand inside her girdle as her skirt falls. His cheeks too are wet with tears. *"Ilsa!"*

"Richard!"

They fall to the floor, grabbing and pulling at each other's clothing. He's trying to get her bra off which is tangled up now with her blouse, she's struggling with his belt, yanking at his black pants, wrenching them open. Buttons fly, straps pop, there's the soft unfocused rip of silk, the jingle of buckles and falling coins, grunts, gasps, whimpers of desire. He strips the tangled skein of underthings away (all these straps and stays—how does she get in and out of this crazy elastic?); she works his pants down past his bucking hips, fumbles with his shoes. *"Your elbow—!"*

"Mmmff!"

"Ah—!"

She pulls his pants and boxer shorts off, crawls round and (he strokes her shimmering buttocks, swept by the light from the airport tower, watching her full breasts sway above him: it's all happening so fast, he'd like to slow it down, repeat some of the better bits—that view of her rippling haunches on her hands and knees just now, for example, like a 22, his lucky number—but there's a great urgency on them, they can't wait) straddles him, easing him into her like a train being guided into a station. *"I luff you, Richard!"* she declares breathlessly, though she seems to be speaking, eyes squeezed shut and breasts heaving, not to him but to the ceiling, if there is one up there. His eyes too are closed now, his hands gripping her soft hips, pulling her down, his breath coming in short anguished snorts, his face puffy and damp with tears. There is, as always, something deeply wounded and vulnerable about the expression on his battered face, framed there against his Persian carpet: Rick Blaine, a man annealed by loneliness and betrayal, but flawed—hopelessly, it seems—by hope itself. He is, in the tragic sense, a true revolutionary: his gaping mouth bespeaks this, the spittle in the corners of his lips, his eyes, open now and staring into some infinite distance not unlike the future, his knitted brow. He heaves upward, impaling her to the very core: *"Oh, Gott!"* she screams, her back arching, mouth agape as though to commence "La Marseillaise."

Now, for a moment, they pause, feeling themselves thus conjoined, his organ luxuriating in the warm tub of her vagina, her enflamed womb closing around his pulsing penis like a mother embracing a lost child. "If you only knew. . . ," she seems to say, though perhaps she has said this before and only now it can be heard. He fondles her breasts; she rips his shirt open, strokes his chest, leans forward to kiss his lips, his nipples. This is not Victor inside her with his long thin rapier, all too rare in its embarrassed visits; this is not Yvonne with her cunning professional muscles, her hollow airy hole. This is love in all its clammy mystery, the ultimate connection, the squishy rub of truth, flesh as a self-consuming message. This is necessity, as in woman needs man, and man must have his mate. Even their identities seem to be dissolving; they have to whisper each other's name from time to time as though in recitative struggle against some ultimate enchantment from which there might be no return. Then slowly she begins to wriggle her hips above him, he to meet her gentle undulations with counterthrusts of his own. They hug each other close, panting, her breasts smashed against him, moving only from the waist down. She slides her thighs between his and squeezes his penis between them, as though to conceal it there, an underground member on the run, wounded but unbowed. He lifts his stockinged feet and plants them behind her knees as though in stirrups, her buttocks above pinching and opening, pinching and opening like a suction pump. And it is true about her vaunted radiance: she seems almost to glow from within, her flexing cheeks haloed in their own dazzling luster.

"It feels so good, Richard! In there . . . I've been so—*ah!*—so lonely. . . !"

"Yeah, me too, kid. *Ngh!* Don't talk."

She slips her thighs back over his and draws them up beside his waist like a child curling around her teddybear, knees against his ribs, her fanny gently bobbing on its pike like a mind caressing a cherished memory. He lies there passively for a moment, stretched out, eyes closed, accepting this warm rhythmical ablution as one might accept a nanny's teasing bath, a mother's care (a care, he's often said, denied him), in all its delicious innocence—or seemingly so: in fact, his whole body is faintly atremble, as though, with great difficulty, shedding the last of its pride and bitterness, its isolate neutrality. Then slowly his own hips begin to rock convulsively under hers, his knees to rise in involuntary surrender. She tongues his ear, her buttocks thumping more vigorously now, kisses his throat, his nose, his scarred lip, then rears up, arching her back, tossing her head back (her hair is looser now, wilder, a flush has crept into the distinctive pallor of her cheeks and throat, and what was before a fierce determination is now raw intensity, what vulnerability now a slack-jawed abandon), plunging him in more deeply than ever, his own buttocks bouncing up off the floor as though trying to take off like the next flight to Lisbon— "Gott in Himmel, *this is fonn!*" she cries. She reaches behind her back to clutch his testicles, he clasps her hand in both of his, his thighs spread, she falls forward, they roll over, he's pounding away now from above (he lacks her famous radiance: if anything his buttocks seem to suck in light, drawing a nostalgic murkiness around them like night fog, signaling a fundamental distance between them, and an irresistible attraction), she's clawing at his back under the white jacket, at his hips, his thighs, her voracious nether mouth leaping up at him from below and sliding back, over and over, like a frantic greased-pole climber. Faster and faster they slap their bodies together, submitting to this fierce rhythm as though to simplify themselves, emitting grunts and whinnies and helpless little farts, no longer Rick Blaine and Ilsa Lund, but some nameless conjunction somewhere between them, time, space, being itself getting redefined by the rapidly narrowing focus of their incandescent passion—then suddenly Rick rears back, his face seeming to puff out like a gourd, Ilsa cries out and kicks upward, crossing her ankles over Rick's clenched buttocks, for a moment they seem almost to float, suspended, unloosed from the earth's gravity, and then—*whumpf!*—they hit the floor again, their bodies continuing to hammer together, though less regularly, plunging, twitching, prolonging this exclamatory dialogue, drawing it out even as the intensity diminishes, even as it becomes more a declaration than a demand, more an inquiry than a declaration. Ilsa's feet uncross, slide slowly to the floor. "Fooff . . . *Gott!*" They lie there, cheek to cheek, clutching each other tightly, gasping for breath, their thighs quivering with the last involuntary spasms, the echoey reverberations, deep in their loins, of pleasure's fading blasts.

"Jesus," Rick wheezes, "I've been saving that one for a goddamn year and a half. . . !"

"It was the best fokk I effer haff," Ilsa replies with a tremulous sigh, and kisses his ear, runs her fingers in his hair. He starts to roll off her, but she clasps him closely: "No . . . wait. . . !" A deeper thicker pleasure, not so ecstatic, yet somehow more moving, seems to well up from far inside her to embrace the swollen visitor snuggled moistly in her womb, once a familiar friend, a comrade loved and trusted, now almost a stranger, like one resurrected from the dead.

"Ah—!" he gasps. God, it's almost like she's milking it! Then she lets go, surrounding him spongily with a kind of warm wet pulsating gratitude. "Ah . . ."

He lies there between Ilsa's damp silky thighs, feeling his weight thicken, his mind soften and spread. His will drains away as if it were some kind of morbid affection, lethargy overtaking him like an invading army. Even his jaw goes slack, his fingers (three sprawl idly on a dark-tipped breast) limp. He wears his snowy white tuxedo jacket still, his shiny black socks, which, together with the parentheses of Ilsa's white thighs, make his melancholy buttocks—beaten in childhood, lashed at sea, run lean in union skirmishes, sunburned in Ethiopia, and shot at in Spain—look gloomier than ever, swarthy and self-pitying, agape now with a kind of heroic sadness. A violent tenderness. These buttocks are, it could be said, what the pose of isolation looks like at its best: proud, bitter, mournful, and, as the prefect of police might have put it, tremendously attractive. Though his penis has slipped out of its vaginal pocket to lie limply like a fat little toe against her slowly pursing lips, she clasps him close still, clinging to something she cannot quite define, something like a spacious dream of freedom, or a monastery garden, or the discovery of electricity. "Do you have a gramophone on, Richard?"

"What—?!" Her question has startled him. His haunches snap shut, his head rears up, snorting, he seems to be reaching for the letters of transit. "Ah . . . no . . ." He relaxes again, letting his weight fall back, though sliding one thigh over hers now, stretching his arms out as though to unkink them, turning his face away. His scrotum bulges up on her thigh like an emblem of his inner serenity and generosity, all too often concealed, much as an authentic decency might shine through a mask of cynicism and despair. He takes a deep breath. (A kiss is just a kiss is what the music is insinuating. A sigh . . .) "That's probably Sam . . ."

She sighs (. . . and so forth), gazing up at the ceiling above her, patterned with overlapping circles of light from the room's lamps and swept periodically by the wheeling airport beacon, coming and going impatiently, yet reliably, like desire itself. "He hates me, I think."

"Sam? No, he's a pal. What I think, he thinks."

"When we came into the bar last night, he started playing 'Luff for Sale.' Effryone turned and looked at me."

"It wasn't the song, sweetheart, it was the way you two were dressed. Nobody in Casablanca—"

"Then he tried to chase me away. He said I was bad luck to you." She can still see the way he rolled his white eyes at her, like some kind of crazy voodoo zombie.

Richard grunts ambiguously. "Maybe you should stop calling him 'boy.' "

Was that it? "But in all the moofies—" Well, a translation problem probably, a difficulty she has known often in her life. Language can sometimes be stiff as a board. Like what's under her now. She loves Richard's relaxed weight on her, the beat of his heart next to her breast, the soft lumpy pouch of his genitals squashed against her thigh, but the floor seems to be hardening under her like some kind of stern Calvinist rebuke and there is a disagreeable airy stickiness between her legs, now that he has slid away from there. "Do you haff a bidet, Richard?"

"Sure, kid." He slides to one side with a lazy grunt, rolls over. He's thinking vaguely about the pleasure he's just had, what it's likely to cost him (he doesn't care), and wondering where he'll find the strength to get up off his ass and go look for a cigarette. He stretches his shirttail down and wipes his crotch with it, nods back over the top of his head. "In there."

She is sitting up, peering between her spread legs. "I am afraid we haff stained your nice carpet, Richard."

"What of it? Put it down as a gesture to love. Want a drink?"

"Yes, that would be good." She leans over and kisses him, her face still flushed and eyes damp, but smiling now, then stands and gathers up an armload of tangled clothing. "Do I smell something burning?"

"What—?!" He rears up. "My goddamn cigarette! I musta dropped it on the couch!" He crawls over, brushes at it: it's gone out, but there's a big hole there now, dark-edged like ringworm. "Shit." He staggers to his feet, stumbles over to the humidor to light up a fresh smoke. Nothing's ever free, he thinks, feeling a bit light-headed. "What's your poison, kid?"

"I haff downstairs been drinking Cointreau," she calls out over the running water in the next room. He pours himself a large whiskey, tosses it down neat (light, sliding by, catches his furrowed brow as he tips his head back: what is wrong?), pours another, finds a decanter of Grand Marnier. She won't know the difference. In Paris she confused champagne with sparkling cider, ordered a Pommard thinking she was getting a rosé, drank gin because she couldn't taste it. He fits the half-burned cigarette between his lips, tucks a spare over his ear, then carries the drinks into the bathroom. She sits, straddling the bidet, churning water up between her legs like the wake of a pleasure boat. The beacon doesn't reach in here: it's as though he's stepped out of its line of sight, but that doesn't make him feel easier (something is nagging at him, has been for some time now). He holds the drink to her mouth for her, and she sips, looking mischievously up at him, one wet hand braced momentarily on his hipbone. Even in Paris she seemed to think drinking was naughtier than sex. Which made her on occasion something of a souse. She tips her chin, and he sets her drink down on the sink. "I wish I didn't luff you so much," she says casually, licking her lips, and commences to work up a lather between her legs with a bar of soap.

"Listen, what did you mean," he asks around the cigarette (this is it, or part of it: he glances back over his shoulder apprehensively, as though to find some answer to his question staring him in the face—or what, from the rear, is passing for his face), "when you said, 'Is this right?' "

"When. . . ?"

"A while ago, when I grabbed your, you know—"

"Oh, I don't know, darling. Yust a strange feeling, I don't exactly remember." She spreads the suds up her smooth belly and down the insides of her thighs, runs the soap up under her behind. "Like things were happening too fast or something."

He takes a contemplative drag on the cigarette, flips the butt into the toilet. "Yeah, that's it." Smoke curls out his nostrils like balloons of speech in a comic strip. "*All* this seems strange somehow. Like something that shouldn't have—"

"Well, I *am* a married woman, Richard."

"I don't mean that." But maybe he does mean that. She's rinsing now, her breasts flopping gaily above her splashing, it's hard to keep his mind on things. But he's not only been pronging some other guy's wife, this is the wife of Victor Laszlo of the International Underground, one of his goddamn heroes. One of the world's. Does that matter? He shoves his free hand in a jacket pocket, having no other, tosses back the drink. "Anyway," he wheezes, "from what you tell me, you were married already when we met in Paris, so that's not—"

"Come here, Richard," Ilsa interrupts with gentle but firm Teutonic insistence. *Komm' hier.* His back straightens, his eyes narrow, and for a moment the old Rick Blaine returns, the lonely American warrior, incorruptible, melancholy, master of his own fate, beholden to no one—but then she reaches forward and, like destiny, takes a hand. "Don't try to escape," she murmurs, pulling him up to the bidet between her knees. "You will neffer succeed."

She continues to hold him with one hand (he is growing there, stretching and filling in her hand with soft warm pulsations, and more than anything else that has happened to her since she came to Casablanca, more even than Sam's song, it is this sensation that takes her back to their days in Paris: wherever they went, from the circus to the movies, from excursion boats to dancehalls, it swelled in her hand, just like this), while soaping him up with the other. "Why are you circumcised, Richard?" she asks, as the engorged head (when it flushes, it seems to flush blue) pushes out between her thumb and index finger. There was something he always said in Paris when it poked up at her like that. She peers wistfully at it, smiling to herself.

"My old man was a sawbones," he says, and takes a deep breath. He sets his empty glass down, reaches for the spare fag. It seems to have vanished. "He thought it was hygienic."

"Fictor still has his. Off course in Europe it is often important not to be mistaken for a Chew." She takes up the fragrant bar of soap (black market, the best, Ferrari gets it for him) and buffs the shaft with it, then thumbs the head with her sudsy hands as though, gently, trying to uncap it. The first day he met her, she opened his pants and jerked him off in his top-down convertible right under the Arc de Triomphe, then, almost without transition, or so it seemed to him, blew him spectacularly in the Bois de Boulogne. He remembers every detail, or anyway the best parts. And it was never—ever—any better than that. Until tonight.

She rinses the soap away, pours the rest of the Grand Marnier (she thinks: Cointreau) over his gleaming organ like a sort of libation, working the excess around as though lightly basting it (he thinks: priming it). A faint sad smile seems to be playing at the corners of her lips. "Say it once, Richard . . ."

"What—?"

She's smiling sweetly, but: is that a tear in her eye? "For old times' sake. Say it . . ."

"Ah." Yes, he'd forgotten. He's out of practice. He grunts, runs his hand down her damp cheek and behind her ear. "Here's lookin' at you, kid . . ."

She puckers her lips and kisses the tip, smiling cross-eyed at it, then, opening her mouth wide, takes it in, all of it at once. "Oh, Christ!" he groans, feeling himself awash in the thick muscular foam of her saliva, "I'm crazy about you, baby!"

"Mmmm!" she moans. He has said that to her before, more than once no doubt (she wraps her arms around his hips under the jacket and hugs him close), but the time she is thinking about was at the cinema one afternoon in Paris. They had gone to see an American detective movie that was popular at the time, but there was a newsreel on before showing the Nazi conquests that month of Copenhagen, Oslo, Luxembourg, Amsterdam, and Brussels. "The Fall of Five Capitals," it was called. And the scenes from Oslo, though brief, showing the Gestapo goose-stepping through the storied streets of her childhood filled her with such terror and nostalgia (something inside her was screaming, "Who *am* I?"), that she reached impulsively for Richard's hand, grabbing what Victor calls "the old fellow" instead. She started to pull her hand back, but he held it there, and the next thing she knew she had her head in his lap, weeping and sucking as though at her dead mother's breast, the terrible roar of the German blitzkrieg pounding in her ears, Richard kneading her nape as her father used to do before he died (and as Richard is doing now, his buttocks knotted up under her arms, his penis fluttering in her mouth like a frightened bird), the Frenchmen in the theater shouting out obscenities, her own heart pounding like cannon fire. "God! I'm crazy about you, baby!" Richard whinnied as he came (now, as his knees buckle against hers and her mouth fills with the shockingly familiar unfamiliarity of his spurting seed, it is just a desperate "Oh fuck! Don't let go. . . !"), and when she sat up, teary-eyed and drooling and gasping for breath (it is not all that easy to breathe now, as he clasps her face close to his hairy belly, whimpering gratefully, his body sagging, her mouth filling), what she saw on the screen were happy Germans, celebrating their victories, taking springtime strolls through overflowing flower and vegetable markets, going to the theater to see translations of Shakespeare, snapping photographs of their children. "Oh Gott," she sniffled then (now she swallows, sucks and swallows, as though to draw out from this almost impalpable essence some vast structure of recollection), "it's too much!" Whereupon the man behind them leaned over and said: "Then try mine, mademoiselle. As you can see, it is not so grand as your Nazi friend's, but here in France, we grow men not pricks!" Richard's French was terrible, but it was good enough to understand "your Nazi friend": he hadn't even put his penis back in his pants (now it slides greasily past her chin, flops down her chest, his buttocks in her hugging arms going soft as butter, like a delicious half-grasped memory losing its clear outlines, melting into mere sensation), but just leapt up and took a swing at the Frenchman. With that, the cinema broke into an uproar with everybody calling everyone else a fascist or a whore. They were thrown out of the theater of course, the police put Richard on their blacklist as an exhibitionist, and they never did get to see the detective movie. Ah well, they could laugh about it then . . .

He sits now on the front lip of the bidet, his knees knuckled under hers, shirttails in the water, his cheek fallen on her broad shoulder, arms loosely around her, feeling wonderfully unwound, mellow as an old tune (which is still there somewhere, moonlight and love songs, same old story—maybe it's coming up through the pipes), needing only a smoke to make things perfect. The one he stuck over his ear is floating in the scummy pool beneath them, he sees. Ilsa idly splashes his drooping organ as though christening it. Only one answer, she once said, peeling off that lovely satin gown of hers like a French letter, will take care of all our questions, and she was right. As always. He's the one who's made a balls-up of things with his complicated moral poses and insufferable pride—a diseased romantic, Louis once called him, and he didn't know the half of it. She's the only realist in town; he's got to start paying attention. Even now she's making sense: "My rump is getting dumb, Richard. Dry me off and let's go back in the other room."

But when he tries to stand, his knees feel like toothpaste, and he has to sit again. Right back in the bidet, as it turns out, dipping his ass like doughnuts in tea. She smiles understandingly, drapes a bath towel around her shoulders, pokes through the medicine cabinet until she finds a jar of Yvonne's cold cream, then takes him by the elbow. "Come on, Richard. You can do it, yust lean on me." Which reminds him (his mind at least is still working, more or less) of a night in Spain, halfway up (or down) Suicide Hill in the Jarama valley, a night he thought was to be his last, when he said that to someone, or someone said it to him. God, what if he'd got it shot off there? And missed this? An expression compounded of hope and anguish, skepticism and awe, crosses his weary face (thirty-eight at Christmas, if Strasser is right—oh mother of God, it *is* going by!), picked up by the wheeling airport beacon. She removes his dripping jacket, his shirt as well, and towels his behind before letting him collapse onto the couch, then crosses to the ornamental table for a cigarette from the humidor. She wears the towel like a cape, her haunches under it glittering as though sequined. She is, as always, a kind of walking light show, no less spectacular from the front as she turns back now toward the sofa, the nubbly texture of the towel contrasting subtly with the soft glow of her throat and breast, the sleek wet gleam of her belly.

She fits two cigarettes in her lips, lights them both (there's a bit

of fumbling with the lighter, she's not very mechanical), and gazing soulfully down at Rick, passes him one of them. He grins.
"Hey, where'd you learn that, kid?" She shrugs enigmatically,
hands him the towel, and steps up between his knees. As he rubs
her breasts, her belly, her thighs with the towel, the cigarette
dangling in his lips, she gazes around at the chalky rough-plas-
tered walls of his apartment, the Moorish furniture with its fili-
grees and inlaid patterns, the little bits of erotic art (there is a
statue of a camel on the sideboard that looks like a man's wet
penis on legs, and a strange nude statuette that might be a boy, or
a girl, or something in between), the alabaster lamps and potted
plants, those slatted wooden blinds, so exotic to her Northern
eyes: he has style, she thinks, rubbing cold cream into her neck
and shoulder with her free hand, he always did have . . .

She lifts one leg for him to dry and then the other, gasping in-
wardly (outwardly, she chokes and wheezes, having inhaled the
cigarette by mistake: he stubs out his own with a sympathetic
grin, takes what is left of hers) when he rubs the towel briskly between them, then she turns and bends over, bracing herself on the
coffee table. Rick, the towel in his hands, pauses a moment, gazing thoughtfully through the drifting cigarette haze at these luminous buttocks, finding something almost otherworldly about
them, like archways to heaven or an image of eternity. Has he
seen them like this earlier tonight? Maybe, he can't remember.
Certainly now he's able to savor the sight, no longer crazed by
rut. They are, quite literally, a dream come true: he has whacked
off to their memory so often during the last year and a half that it
almost feels more appropriate to touch himself than this present
manifestation. As he reaches toward them with the towel, he
seems to be crossing some strange threshold, as though passing
from one medium into another. He senses the supple buoyancy of
them bouncing back against his hand as he wipes them, yet,
though flesh, they remain somehow immaterial, untouchable even
when touched, objects whose very presence is a kind of absence.
If Rick Blaine were to believe in angels, Ilsa's transcendent bottom is what they would look like.

"Is this how you, uh, imagined things turning out tonight?" he asks around the butt, smoke curling out his nose like thought's reek. Her cheeks seem to pop alight like his Café Américain sign each time the airport beacon sweeps past, shifting slightly like a sequence of film frames. Time itself may be like that, he knows: not a ceaseless flow, but a rapid series of electrical leaps across tiny gaps between discontinuous bits. It's what he likes to call his link-and-claw theory of time, though of course the theory is not his . . .

"Well, it may not be perfect, Richard, but it is better than if I haff shot you, isn't it?"

"No, I meant . . ." Well, let it be. She's right, it beats eating a goddamn bullet. In fact it beats anything he can imagine. He douses his cigarette in the wet towel, tosses it aside, wraps his arms around her thighs and pulls her buttocks (he is still thinking about time as a pulsing sequence of film frames, and not so much about the frames, their useless dated content, as the gaps between: infinitesimally small when looked at two-dimensionally, yet in their third dimension as deep and mysterious as the cosmos) toward his face, pressing against them like a child trying to see through a foggy window. He kisses and nibbles at each fresh-washed cheek (and what if one were to slip *between* two of those frames? he wonders—), runs his tongue into (—where would he be then?) her anus, kneading the flesh on her pubic knoll between his fingers all the while like little lumps of stiff taffy. She raises one knee up onto the cushions, then the other, lowering her elbows to the floor (oh! she thinks as the blood rushes in two directions at once, spreading into her head and sex as though filling empty frames, her heart the gap between: what a strange dizzying dream time is!), thus lifting to his contemplative scrutiny what looks like a clinging sea anemone between her thighs, a thick woolly pod, a cloven chinchilla, open purse, split fruit. But it is not the appearance of it that moves him (except to the invention of these fanciful catalogues), it is the smell. It is this which catapults him suddenly and wholly back to Paris, a Paris he'd lost until this moment (she is not in Paris, she is in some vast dimensionless region she associates with childhood, a nighttime glow in her midsummer room, featherbedding between her legs) but now has back again. Now and for all time. As he runs his tongue up and down the spongy groove, pinching the lips tenderly between his tongue and stiff upper lip (an old war wound), feeling it engorge, pulsate, almost pucker up to kiss him back, he seems to see—as though it were fading in on the blank screen of her gently rolling bottom—that night at her apartment in Paris when she first asked him to "Kiss me, Richard, here. My other mouth wants to luff you, too . . ." He'd never done that before. He had been all over the world, had fought in wars, battled cops, been jailed and tortured, hid out in whorehouses, parachuted out of airplanes, had eaten and drunk just about everything, had been blown off the decks of ships, killed more men than he'd like to count, and had banged every kind and color of woman on earth, but he had never tasted one of these things before. Other women had sucked him off, of course, before Ilsa nearly caused him to wreck his car that day in the Bois de Boulogne, but he had always thought of that as a service due him, something he'd paid for in effect—he was the man, after all. But reciprocation, sucking back—well, that always struck him as vaguely queer, something guys, manly guys anyway, didn't do. That night, though, he'd had a lot of champagne and he was—this was the simple truth, and it was an experience as exotic to Rick Blaine as the taste of a cunt—madly in love. He had been an unhappy misfit all his life, at best a romantic drifter, at worst and in the eyes of most a sleazy gunrunner and chickenshit mercenary (though God knows he'd hoped for more), a whoremonger and brawler and miserable gutter drunk: nothing like Ilsa Lund had ever happened to him, and he could hardly believe it was happening to him that night. His immediate reaction—he admits this, sucking greedily at it now (she is galloping her father's horse through the woods of the north, canopy-dark and sunlight-blinding at the same time, pushing the beast beneath her, racing toward what she believed to be God's truth, flushing through her from the saddle up as eternity might when the saints were called), while watching himself, on the cinescreen of her billowing behind, kneel to it that first time like an atheist falling squeamishly into conversion—was not instant rapture. No, like olives, home brew, and Arab cooking, it took a little getting used to. But she taught him how to stroke the vulva with his tongue, where to find the nun's cap ("my little sister," she called it, which struck him as odd) and how to draw it out, how to use his fingers, nose, chin, even his hair and ears, and the more he practiced for her sake, the more he liked it for his own, her pleasure (he could *see* it: it bloomed right under his nose, filling his grimy life with colors he'd never even thought of before!) augmenting his, until he found his appetite for it almost insatiable. God, the boys on the block back in New York would laugh their asses off to see how far he'd fallen! And though he has tried others since, it is still the only one he really likes. Yvonne's is terrible, bitter and pomaded (she seems to sense this, gets no pleasure from it at all, often turns fidgety and mean when he goes down on her, even had a kind of biting, scratching fit once: "Don' you lak to *fuck?*" she'd screamed), which is the main reason he's lost interest in her. That and her hairy legs.

His screen is shrinking (her knees have climbed to his shoulders, scrunching her hips into little bumps and bringing her shoulderblades into view, down near the floor, where she is gasping and whimpering and sucking the carpet), but his vision of the past is expanding, as though her pumping cheeks were a chubby bellows, opening and closing, opening and closing, inflating his memories. Indeed, he no longer needs a screen for them, for it is not this or that conquest that he recalls now, this or that event, not what she wore or what she said, what he said, but something more profound than that, something experienced in the way that a blind man sees or an amputee touches. Texture returns to him, ambience, impressions of radiance, of coalescence, the foamy taste of the ineffable on his tongue, the downy nap of timelessness, the tooth of now. All this he finds in Ilsa's juicy bouncing cunt—and more: love's pungent illusions of consubstantiation and infinitude (oh, he knows what he lost that day in the rain in the Gare de Lyon!), the bittersweet fall into actuality, space's secret folds wherein one might lose one's ego, one's desperate sense of isolation, Paris, rediscovered here as pure aura, effervescent and allusive, La Belle Aurore as immanence's theater, sacred showplace—

Oh hell, he thinks as Ilsa's pounding hips drive him to his back on the couch, her thighs slapping against his ears (as she rises, her blood in riptide against her mounting excitement, the airport beacon touching her in its passing like bursts of inspiration, she thinks: childhood is a place apart, needing the adult world to exist at all: without Victor there could *be* no Rick!—and then she cannot think at all), La Belle Aurore! She broke his goddamn heart at La Belle Aurore. "Kiss me," she said, holding herself with both hands as though to keep the pain from spilling out down there, "one last time," and he did, for her, Henri didn't care, merde alors, the Germans were coming anyway, and the other patrons thought it was just part of the entertainment; only Sam was offended and went off to the john till it was over. And then she left him. Forever. Or anyway until she turned up here a night ago with Laszlo. God, he remembers everything about that day in the Belle Aurore, what she was wearing, what the Germans were wearing, what Henri was wearing. It was not an easy day to forget. The Germans were at the very edge of the city, they were bombing the bejesus out of the place and everything was literally falling down around their ears (she's smothering him now with her bucking arse, her scissoring thighs: he heaves her over onto her back and pushes his arms between her thighs to spread them); they'd had to crawl over rubble and dead bodies, push through barricades, just to reach the damned café. No chance to get out by car, he was lucky there was enough left in his "F.Y. Fund" to buy them all train tickets. And then the betrayal: "I can' find her, Mr. Richard. She's checked outa de hotel. But dis note come jus' after you lef'!" Oh shit, even now it makes him cry. "I cannot go with you or ever see you again." In perfect Palmer Method handwriting, as though to exult in her power over him. He kicked poor Sam's ass up and down that train all the way to Marseilles, convinced it was somehow his fault. Even a hex maybe, that day he could have believed anything. Now, with her hips bouncing frantically up against his mouth, her bush grown to an astonishing size, the lips out and flapping like flags, the trench between them awash in a fragrant ooze like oily air, he lifts his head and asks: "Why weren't you honest with me? Why did you keep your marriage a secret?"

"Oh Gott, Richard! Not *now*—!"

She's right, it doesn't seem the right moment for it, but then nothing has seemed right since she turned up in this godforsaken town: it's almost as though two completely different places, two completely different times, are being forced to mesh, to intersect where no intersection is possible, causing a kind of warp in the universe. In his own private universe anyway. He gazes down on this lost love, this faithless wife, this trusting child, her own hands between her legs now, her hips still jerking out of control ("Please, Richard!" she is begging softly through clenched teeth, tears in her eyes), thinking: It's still a story without an ending. But more than that: the beginning and middle bits aren't all there either. Her face is drained as though all the blood has rushed away to other parts, but her throat between the heaving white breasts is almost literally alight with its vivid blush. He touches it, strokes the soft bubbles to either side, watching the dark little nipples rise like patriots—and suddenly the answer to all his questions seems (yet another one, that is—answers, in the end, are easy) to suggest itself. "Listen kid, would it be all right if I—?"

"Oh yes! yes!—*but hurry!*"

He finds the cold cream (at last! he is so slow!), lathers it on, and slips into her cleavage, his knees over her shoulders like a yoke. She guides his head back into that tropical explosion between her legs, then clasps her arms around his hips, already beginning to thump at her chest like a resuscitator, popping little gasps from her throat. She tries to concentrate on his bouncing buttocks, but they communicate to her such a touching blend of cynicism and honesty, weariness and generosity, that they nearly break her heart, making her more light-headed than ever. The dark little hole between them bobs like a lonely survivor in a tragically divided world. It is he! "Oh Gott!" she whimpers. And she! The tension between her legs is almost unbearable. "I can't fight it anymore!" Everything starts to come apart. She feels herself falling as though through some rift in the universe (she cannot wait for him, and anyway, where she is going he cannot follow), out of time and matter into some wondrous radiance, the wheeling beacon flashing across her stricken vision now like intermittent star bursts, the music swelling, *everything* swelling, her eyes bursting, ears popping, teeth ringing in their sockets—"Oh Richard! Oh fokk! *I luff you so much!*"

He plunges his face deep into Ilsa's ambrosial pudding, lapping at its sweet sweat, feeling her loins snap and convulse violently around him, knowing that with a little inducement she can spasm like this for minutes on end, and meanwhile pumping away between her breasts now like a madman, no longer obliged to hold back, seeking purely his own pleasure. This pleasure is tempered only by (and maybe enhanced by as well) his pity for her husband, that heroic sonuvabitch. God, Victor Laszlo is almost a father figure to him, really. And while Laszlo is off at the underground meeting in the Caverne du Roi, no doubt getting his saintly ass shot to shit, here he is—Rick Blaine, the Yankee smart aleck and general jerk-off—safely closeted off in his rooms over the town saloon, tit-fucking the hero's wife, his callous nose up her own royal grotto like an advance scout for a squad of storm troopers. It's not fair, goddamn it, he thinks, and laughs at this even as he comes, squirting jism down her sleek belly and under his own, his head locked in her clamped thighs, her arms hugging him tightly as though to squeeze the juices out.

He is lying, completely still, his face between Ilsa's flaccid thighs, knees over her shoulders, arms around her lower body, which sprawls loosely now beneath him. He can feel her hands resting lightly on his hips, her warm breath against his leg. He doesn't remember when they stopped moving. Maybe he's been sleeping. Has he dreamt it all? No, he shifts slightly and feels the spill of semen, pooled gummily between their conjoined navels.

His movement wakes Ilsa: she snorts faintly, sighs, kisses the inside of his leg, strokes one buttock idly. "That soap smells nice," she murmurs. "I bet effry girl in Casablanca wishes to haff a bath here."

"Yeah, well, I run it as a kind of public service," he grunts, chewing the words around a strand or two of pubic hair. He's always told Louis—and anyone else who wanted to know—that he sticks his neck out for nobody. But in the end, shit, he thinks, I stick it out for everybody. "I'm basically a civic-minded guy."

Cynic-minded, more like, she thinks, but keeps the thought to herself. She cannot risk offending him, not just now. She is still returning from wherever it is orgasm has taken her, and it has been an experience so profound and powerful, yet so remote from its immediate cause—his muscular tongue at the other end of this morosely puckered hole in front of her nose—that it has left her feeling very insecure, unsure of who or what she is, or even where. She knows of course that her role as the well-dressed wife of a courageous underground leader is just pretense, that beneath this charade she is certainly someone—or something—else. Richard's lover, for example. Or a little orphan girl who lost her mother, father, and adoptive aunt, all before she'd even started menstruating—that's who she often is, or feels like she is, especially at moments like this. But if her life as Victor Laszlo's wife is not real, are these others any more so? Is she one person, several—or no one at all? What was that thought she'd had about childhood? She lies there, hugging Richard's hairy cheeks (are they Richard's? are they cheeks?), her pale face framed by his spraddled legs, trying to puzzle it all out. Since the moment she arrived in Casablanca, she and Richard have been trying to tell each other stories, not very funny stories, as Richard has remarked, but maybe not very true ones either. Maybe memory itself is a kind of trick, something that turns illusion into reality and makes the real world vanish before everyone's eyes like magic. One can certainly sink away there and miss everything, she knows. Hasn't Victor, the wise one, often warned her of that? But Victor is a hero. Maybe the real world is too much for most people. Maybe making up stories is a way to keep them all from going insane. A tear forms in the corner of one eye. She blinks (and what are these unlikely configurations called "Paris" and "Casablanca," where in all the universe *is* she, and what is "where"?), and the tear trickles into the hollow between cheekbone and nose, then bends its course toward the middle of her cheek. There is a line in their song (yes, it is still there, tinkling away somewhere like mice in the walls: is someone trying to drive her crazy?) that goes, "This day and age we're living in gives cause for apprehension,/With speed and new invention and things like third dimension . . ." She always thought that was a stupid mistake of the lyricist, but now she is not so sure. For the real mystery—she sees this now, or *feels* it rather—is not the fourth dimension as she'd always supposed (the tear stops halfway down her cheek, begins to fade), or the third either for that matter . . . but the *first*.

"You never finished answering my question . . ."

There is a pause. Perhaps she is daydreaming. "What question, Richard?"

"A while ago. In the bathroom . . ." He, too, has been mulling over recent events, wondering not only about the events themselves (wondrous in their own right, of course: he's not enjoyed multiple orgasms like this since he hauled his broken-down blacklisted ass out of Paris a year and a half ago, and that's just for starters), but also about their "recentness": When did they really happen? Is "happen" the right word, or were they more like fleeting conjunctions with the Absolute, that *other* Other, boundless and immutable as number? And, if so, what now is "when"? How much time has elapsed, for example, since he opened the door and found her in this room? Has *any* time elapsed? "I asked you what you meant when you said, 'Is this right?' "

"Oh, Richard, I don't know what's right any longer." She lifts one thigh in front of his face, as though to erase his dark imaginings. He strokes it, thinking: well, what the hell, it probably doesn't amount to a hill of beans, anyway. "Do you think I can haff another drink now?"

"Sure, kid. Why not." He sits up beside her, shakes the butt out of the damp towel, wipes his belly off, hands the towel to her. "More of the same?"

"Champagne would be nice, if it is possible. It always makes me think of Paris . . . and you . . ."

"You got it, sweetheart." He pushes himself to his feet and thumps across the room, pausing at the humidor to light up a fresh smoke. "If there's any left. Your old man's been going through my stock like Vichy water." Not for the first time, he has the impression of being watched. Laszlo? Who knows, maybe the underground meeting was just a ruse; it certainly seemed like a dumb thing to do on the face of it, especially with Strasser in town. There's a bottle of champagne in his icebox, okay, but no ice. He touches the bottle: not cold, but cool enough. It occurs to him the sonuvabitch might be out on the balcony right now, taking it all in, he and all his goddamn underground. Europeans can be pretty screwy, especially these rich stiffs with titles. As he carries the champagne and glasses over to the coffee table, the cigarette like a dart between his lips, his bare ass feels suddenly both hot and chilly at the same time. "Does your husband ever get violent?" he asks around the smoke and snaps the metal clamp off the champagne bottle, takes a grip on the cork.

"No. He has killed some people, but he is not fiolent." She is rubbing her tummy off, smiling thoughtfully. The light from the airport beacon, wheeling past, picks up a varnishlike glaze still between her breasts, a tooth's wet twinkle in her open mouth, an unwonted shine on her nose. The cork pops, champagne spews out over the table top, some of it getting into the glasses. This seems to suggest somehow a revelation. Or another memory. The tune, as though released, rides up once more around them. "Gott, Richard," she sighs, pushing irritably to her feet. "That music is getting on my nerfs!"

"Yeah, I know." It's almost as bad in its way as the German blitzkrieg hammering in around their romance in Paris—sometimes it seemed to get right between their embraces. Gave him a goddamn headache. Now the music is doing much the same thing, even trying to tell them when to kiss and when not to. He can stand it, though, he thinks, tucking the cigarette back in his lips, if she can. He picks up the two champagne glasses, offers her one. "Forget it, kid. Drown it out with this." He raises his glass. "Uh, here's lookin'——"

She gulps it down absently, not waiting for his toast. "And that light from the airport," she goes on, batting at it as it passes as though to shoo it away. "How can you effer sleep here?"

"No one's supposed to sleep well in Casablanca," he replies with a worldly grimace. It's his best expression, he knows, but she isn't paying any attention. He stubs out the cigarette, refills her glass, blowing a melancholy whiff of smoke over it. "Hey, kid here's——"

"No, wait!" she insists, her ear cocked. "*Is* it?"

"Is what?" Ah well, forget the fancy stuff. He drinks off the champagne in his glass, reaches down for a refill.

"Time. Is it going by? Like the song is saying?"

He looks up, startled. "That's funny, I was just——!"

"What time do you haff, Richard?"

He sets the bottle down, glances at his empty wrist. "I dunno. My watch must have got torn off when we . . ."

"Mine is gone, too."

They stare at each other a moment, Rick scowling slightly in the old style, Ilsa's lips parted as though saying "story," or "glory." Then the airport beacon sweeps past like a prompter, and Rick, blinking, says: "Wait a minute—there's a clock down in the bar!" He strides purposefully over to the door in his stocking feet, pausing there a moment, one hand on the knob, to take a deep breath. "I'll be right back," he announces, then opens the door and (she seems about to call out to him) steps out on the landing. He steps right back in again. He pushes the door closed, leans against it, his face ashen. "They're all down there," he says.

"What? Who's down there?"

"Karl, Sam, Abdul, that Norwegian——"

"Fictor?!"

"Yes, everybody! Strasser, those goddamn Bulgarians, Sasha, Louis—"

"Yffonne?"

Why the hell did she ask about Yvonne? "I said everybody! They're just standing down there! Like they're waiting for something! But . . . for what?!" He can't seem to stop his goddamn voice from squeaking. He wants to remain cool and ironically detached, cynical even, because he knows it's expected of him, not least of all by himself, but he's still shaken by what he's seen down in the bar. Of course it might help if he had his pants on. At least he'd have some pockets to shove his hands into. For some reason, Ilsa is staring at his crotch, as though the real horror of it all were to be found there. Or maybe she's trying to see through to the silent crowd below. "It's, I dunno, like the place has sprung a goddamn leak or something!"

She crosses her hands to her shoulders, pinching her elbows in, hugging her breasts. She seems to have gone flat-footed, her feet splayed, her bottom, lost somewhat in the slatted shadows, drooping, her spine bent. "A leak?" she asks meaninglessly in her soft Scandinavian accent. She looks like a swimmer out of water in chilled air. Richard, slumping against the far door, stares at her as though at a total stranger. Or perhaps a mirror. He seems older somehow, tired, his chest sunken and belly out, legs bowed, his genitals shriveled up between them like dried fruit. It is not a beautiful sight. Of course Richard is not a beautiful man. He is short and bad-tempered and rather smashed up. Victor calls him riffraff. He says Richard makes him feel greasy. And it is true, there is something common about him. Around Victor she always feels crisp and white, but around Richard like a sweating pig. So how did she get mixed up with him, in the first place? Well, she was lonely, she had nothing, not even hope, and he seemed so happy when she took hold of his penis. As Victor has often said, each of us has a destiny, for good or for evil, and her destiny was Richard. Now that destiny seems confirmed—or sealed—by all those people downstairs. "They are not waiting for anything," she says, as the realization comes to her. It is over.

Richard grunts in reply. He probably hasn't heard her. She feels a terrible sense of loss. He shuffles in his black socks over to the humidor. "Shit, even the fags are gone," he mutters gloomily. "Why'd you have to come to Casablanca anyway, goddamn it; there are other places . . ." The airport beacon, sliding by, picks up an expression of intense concentration on his haggard face. She knows he is trying to understand what cannot be understood, to resolve what has no resolution. Americans are like that. In Paris he was always wondering how it was they kept getting from one place to another so quickly. "It's like everything is all speeded up," he would gasp, reaching deliriously between her legs as her apartment welled up around them. Now he is probably wondering why there seems to be no place to go and why time suddenly is just about all they have. He is an innocent man, after all; this is probably his first affair.

"I would not haff come if I haff known . . ." She releases her shoulders, picks up her ruffled blouse (the buttons are gone), pulls it on like a wrap. As the beacon wheels by, the room seems to expand with light as though it were breathing. "Do you see my skirt? It was here, but—is it getting dark or something?"

"I mean, of all the gin joints in all the towns in all the—!" He pauses, looks up. "What did you say?"

"I said, is it—?"

"Yeah, I know . . ."

They gaze about uneasily. "It seems like effry time that light goes past . . ."

"Yeah . . ." He stares at her, slumped there at the foot of the couch, working her garter belt like rosary beads, looking like somebody had just pulled her plug. "The world will always welcome lovers," the music is suggesting, not so much in mockery as in sorrow. He's thinking of all those people downstairs, so hushed, so motionless: it's almost how he feels inside. Like something dying. Or something dead revealed. Oh shit. Has this happened before? Ilsa seems almost wraithlike in the pale staticky light, as though she were wearing her own ghost on her skin. And which is it he's been in love with? he wonders. He sees she is trembling, and a tear slides down the side of her nose, or seems to, it's hard to tell. He feels like he's going blind. "Listen. Maybe if we started over . . ."

"I'm too tired, Richard . . ."

"No, I mean, go back to where you came in, see—the letters of transit and all that. Maybe we made some kinda mistake, I dunno, like when I put my hands on your jugs or something, and if—"

"A mistake? You think putting your hands on my yugs was a mistake—?"

"Don't get offended, sweetheart. I only meant—"

"Maybe my bringing my yugs *here* tonight was a mistake! Maybe my not shooting the *trigger* was a mistake!"

"Come on, don't get your tail in an uproar, goddamn it! I'm just trying to—"

"Oh, what a fool I was to fall . . . to fall . . ."

"Jesus, Ilsa, are you crying. . . ? Ilsa. . . ?" He sighs irritably. He is never going to understand women. Her head is bowed as though in resignation: one has seen her like this often when Laszlo is near. She seems to be staring at the empty buttonholes in her blouse. Maybe she's stupider than he thought. When the dimming light swings past, tears glint in the corners of her eyes, little points of light in the gathering shadows on her face. "Hey, dry up, kid! All I want you to do is go over there by the curtains where you were when I—"

"Can I tell you a . . . story, Richard?"

"Not *now*, Ilsa! Christ! The light's almost gone and—"

"Anyway, it wouldn't work."

"What?"

"Trying to do it all again. It wouldn't work. It wouldn't be the same. I won't even haff my girdle on."

"That doesn't matter. Who's gonna know? Come on, we can at least—"

"No, Richard. It is impossible. You are different, I am different. You haff cold cream on your penis—"

"But—!"

"My makeup is gone, there are stains on the carpet. And I

would need the pistol—how could we effer find it in the dark? No, it's useless, Richard. Belief me. Time goes by."

"But maybe that's just it . . ."

"Or what about your tsigarette? Eh? Can you imagine going through that without your tsigarette? Richard? I am laughing! Where are you, Richard . . . ?"

"Take it easy, I'm over here. By the balcony. Just lemme think."

"Efen the airport light has stopped."

"Yeah. I can't see a fucking thing out there."

"Well, you always said you wanted a wow finish . . . Maybe . . ."

"What?"

"What?"

"What did you say?"

"I said, maybe this is . . . you know, what we always wanted . . . Like a dream come true . . ."

"Speak up, kid. It's getting hard to hear you."

"I said, *when we are fokking—*"

"Nah, that won't do any good, sweetheart, I know that now. We gotta get back into the goddamn world somehow. If we don't, we'll regret it. Maybe not today—"

"What? We'll forget it?"

"No, I said—"

"What?"

"Never mind."

"Forget what, Richard?"

"I said I think I shoulda gone fishing with Sam when I had the chance."

"I can't seem to hear you . . ."

"No, wait a minute! Maybe you're right! Maybe going back isn't the right idea . . ."

"Richard . . . ?"

"Instead, maybe we gotta think ahead . . ."

"Richard, I am afraid . . ."

"Yeah, like you could sit there on the couch, see, we've been fucking, that's all right, who cares, now we're having some champagne—"

"I think I am *already* forgetting . . ."

"And you can tell me that story you've been wanting to tell—are you listening? A good story, that may do it—anything that *moves!* And meanwhile, lemme think, I'll, let's see, I'll sit down—no, I'll sort of lean here in the doorway and—*oof!*—shit! I think they moved it!"

"Richard . . . ?"

"Who the hell rearranged the—*ungh!*—goddamn geography?"

"Richard, it's a crazy world . . ."

"Ah, here! this feels like it. Something like it. Now what was I—? Right! You're telling a story, so, uh, I'll say . . ."

"But wherever you are . . ."

"*And then*—? Yeah, that's good. It's almost like I'm remembering this. You've stopped, see, but I want you to go on, I want you to keep spilling what's on your mind, I'm filling in all the blanks . . ."

". . . whatever happens . . ."

"So I say: *And then*—? C'mon, kid, can you hear me? Remember all those people downstairs! They're depending on us! Just think it: if you think it, you'll do it! *And then*—?"

". . . I want you to know . . ."

"*And then* . . . ? Oh shit, Ilsa . . . ? Where are you? And then . . . ?"

". . . I luff you . . ."

"And then . . . ? Ilsa . . . ? And *then* . . . ?"

About the Author

Robert Coover was born in Iowa in 1932. His first novel, *The Origin of the Brunists*, was the winner of the 1966 William Faulkner Award. His other works include *The Universal Baseball Association, J. Henry Waugh, Prop., Pricksongs & Descants, A Theological Position, The Public Burning, A Political Fable, Spanking the Maid*, and *Gerald's Party*. Coover lives with his wife in Providence, Rhode Island, where he teaches at Brown University.

"We are doomed, Professor!" cries the opening voice in this alarmingly inventive collection of short fictions, Robert Coover's first such volume since his internationally acclaimed *Pricksongs & Descants* of 1969. "*The planet is rushing madly toward earth and no human power can stop it!*"

This onrushing planet is not unlike Coover's own prodigious imagination, overtaking us here with a force that is both threatening and spectacular, deeply disturbing yet marvelously entertaining. In this volume he offers us, in all its magic and variety, *A Night at the Movies*, complete with previews of coming attractions, cartoons, the weekly serial, a travelogue, a musical interlude, other selected short subjects, and three full-length features covering that movie-poster spectrum of "the sum total of all human emotions": from *Adventure!* to *Comedy!* to *Romance!* There is even an intermission—though, as always with this master of metafiction, things are not always what they seem. "You can," as the movie advertisements used to say, "expect the unexpected."

Readers of Coover's previous books know this all too well. From *The Origin of the Brunists* and *The Universal Baseball Association, J. Henry Waugh, Prop.*, through *The Public Burning*, *Spanking the Maid*, and *Gerald's Party*, Coover has been at the center of literary, political, and intellectual controversy. While acknowledging him as one of the masters of his generation, critics have described his books as "dangerous," "fiendish," "heretical," and (*The New York Times Book Review*) "work of the purest, unremitting malevolence."

A Night at the Movies is no exception. Coover may conceal a tribute to Buster Keaton here,